George Payn Quackenbos

First Lessons in Composition

George Payn Quackenbos

First Lessons in Composition

Reprint of the original, first published in 1883.

1st Edition 2024 | ISBN: 978-3-38531-523-5

Verlag (Publisher): Outlook Verlag GmbH, Zeilweg 44, 60439 Frankfurt, Deutschland
Vertretungsberechtigt (Authorized to represent): E. Roepke, Zeilweg 44, 60439 Frankfurt, Deutschland
Druck (Print): Books on Demand GmbH, In de Tarpen 42, 22848 Norderstedt, Deutschland

FIRST LESSONS·

IN

COMPOSITION,

IN WHICH THE PRINCIPLES OF THE ART ARE DEVELOPED IN
CONNECTION WITH THE PRINCIPLES OF

GRAMMAR;

EMBRACING

FULL DIRECTIONS ON THE SUBJECT OF PUNCTUATION;

WITH COPIOUS EXERCISES.

BY G. P. QUACKENBOS, LL. D.,

PRINCIPAL OF "THE COLLEGIATE SCHOOL," N. Y.; AUTHOR OF "ADVANCED
COURSE OF COMPOSITION AND RHETORIC," "AN ENGLISH
GRAMMAR," "ILLUSTRATED SCHOOL HISTORY
OF THE UNITED STATES," ETC.

TWO HUNDREDTH THOUSAND.

NEW YORK:
D. APPLETON AND COMPANY,
1, 3, AND 5 BOND STREET.
1883.

By the same Author :

A PRIMARY ARITHMETIC. Handsomely illustrated. 16mo, 108 pages. 20 cents.

AN ELEMENTARY ARITHMETIC. 12mo, 144 pages. 35 cents.

A HIGHER ARITHMETIC. A comprehensive text-book on the science of Arithmetic and its practical applications ; specially designed as an aid in preparing for the counting-house. 12mo, 420 pages. $1.00.

KEY TO HIGHER ARITHMETIC. 12mo, 96 pages. 60 cents.

A MENTAL ARITHMETIC. Designed to impart readiness in mental calculations, and extending them to the various operations needed in business life. 16mo, 168 pages. 32 cents.

KEY TO PRACTICAL ARITHMETIC. 12mo, 72 pages. 18 cents.

FIRST BOOK IN GRAMMAR. 16mo, 120 pages. 40 cents.

AN ENGLISH GRAMMAR. 12mo, 288 pages. 72 cents.

FIRST LESSONS IN COMPOSITION. In which the Principles of the Art are developed in connection with the Principles of Grammar. 12mo. 182 pages. 80 cents.

ADVANCED COURSE OF COMPOSITION AND RHETORIC. A Series of Practical Lessons on the Origin, History, and Peculiarities of the English Language, Punctuation, Taste, the Pleasures of the Imagination, Figures, Style and its Essential Properties, Criticism, and the various Departments of Prose and Poetical Composition. Illustrated with copious Exercises. 12mo, 450 pages. $1.30.

ELEMENTARY HISTORY OF THE UNITED STATES. With numerous Illustrations and Maps. 12mo, 216 pages. 60 cents.

ILLUSTRATED SCHOOL HISTORY OF THE UNITED STATES. Embracing a full Account of the Aborigines, Biographical Notices of Distinguished Men, numerous Maps, Plans of Battle-fields, and Pictorial Illustrations. 12mo, 588 pages. $1.20.

A NATURAL PHILOSOPHY. Embracing the most recent Discoveries in Physics. Adapted to use with or without Apparatus, and accompanied with Practical Exercises and 335 Illustrations. New edition, revised and brought in all respects up to date. 12mo, 450 pages. $1.50.

PREFACE.

A County Superintendent of common schools, speaking of the important branch of composition, in a communication bearing date July 27, 1844, uses the following language: " For a long time I have noticed with regret the almost entire neglect of the art of original composition in our common schools, and the want of a proper text-book upon this essential branch of education. Hundreds graduate from our common schools with no well-defined ideas of the construction of our language." The writer might have gone further, and said that multitudes graduate, not only from common schools, but from some of our best private institutions, utterly destitute of all practical acquaintance with the subject ; that to many such the composition of a simple letter is an irksome, to some an almost impossible, task. Yet the reflecting mind must admit that it is only this practical application of grammar that renders that art useful — that parsing is secondary to composing, and the analysis of our language almost unimportant when compared with its synthesis.

One great reason of the neglect noticed above, has, no doubt, been the want of a suitable text-book on the subject. During the years of the author's experience as a teacher, he has examined, and practically tested, the various works on composition with which he has met : the result has been a conviction that, while there are several publications well calculated to advance pupils at the age of fifteen or sixteen, there is not one suited to the comprehension of those between nine and twelve ; at which time it is his decided opinion this branch should be taken up. Heretofore, the teacher has been obliged either to make the scholar labor through a work entirely too difficult for him, to give him exercises not founded on any regular system, or to abandon the branch altogether—and the disadvantages of either of these courses are at once apparent.

It is this conviction, founded on the experience not only of the author, but of many other teachers with whom he has consulted, that has led to the production of the work now offered to the public. It claims to be a first-book in composition, and is intended to initiate the beginner, by easy and pleasant steps, into that all-important, but hitherto generally neglected, art.

A brief account of the plan and scope of the work may not be out of place. It presupposes no knowledge of grammar, and is intended to be put into a pupil's hands, as a first-book in grammar, at whatever age it is deemed best for him to commence that study ; say from nine to twelve years, according to the degree of intellectual development. In the first fifty pages, by means of lessons on the inductive system, and copious exercises under each, he is made familiar with the nature and *use* of the different parts of speech, so as to be able to recognize them at once, and to supply them when a sentence is rendered incomplete by their omission. After this, he is prepared to take up a more difficult treatise on grammar ; while in this work he is led to consider the different kinds of clauses and sentences, and is thus prepared for punctuation, a subject not generally treated in elementary books with the consideration which its importance demands. The rules for punctuation have been condensed, arranged on a new plan, and, it is hoped, rendered intelligible to all. Directions on the subject of capital letters follow. A few pages are next devoted to rules, explanations, and examples, for the purpose of enabling the pupil to form and spell correctly such derivative words as *having*, *debarring*, *chatted*, and the like, which are not to be found in dictionaries, and regarding which the pupil is apt to be led astray by the fact that a change is made in the primitive word before the addition of a suffix.

This done, the scholar is prepared to express thoughts in his own language, and he is now required to write sentences of every kind, a word being given to suggest an idea for each: he is taught to vary them by means of different arrangement and modes of expression ; to analyze compound sentences into simple ones, and to combine simple sentences into compound. Several lessons are then devoted to the various kinds of style. The essential properties, purity, propriety, precision, clearness, strength, harmony, and unity, are next treated, examples for correction being presented under each. The different kinds of composition follow, and, proper selections having been first given as specimens, the pupil is required to compose successively letters, descriptions, narrations, biographical sketches, essays, and argumentative discourses. After this, the three principal figures receive attention ; and the work closes with a list of subjects carefully selected, arranged under their proper heads, and in such a way that the increase in difficulty is very gradual. The author has aimed throughout to awaken thought in the pupil, to discipline his mind, and by precept and practice to make him acquainted with the construction of his native tongue.

The distinctive features of the work may be briefly enumer-ated as follows: the development of the principles of compo-sition in connection with those of grammar; the easy steps by which it proceeds according to the inductive system; the illus-tration of every point with exercises, not taken, as has hitherto been the general practice, from the time-honored text-book of Murray; the method of analyzing subjects; and the frequency of reviews. Suggestions are scattered through the book, to which it may be well for the teacher to attend. The pupil should, in all cases, prepare himself to answer the questions in each lesson, before he proceeds to the exercise.

With these brief remarks the author commits his work to his professional brethren, respectfully asking them to submit it to that practical trial which is, after all, the only true test of a school-book's value.

New York, *Jan. 1st*, 1851.

CONTENTS.

8   CONTENTS.

FIRST LESSONS IN COMPOSITION.

LESSON I.

LETTERS, VOWELS, CONSONANTS, SYLLABLES.

WHAT is a Letter?

A **Letter** is a character used to represent a sound of the human voice.

How many letters are there in the English language?

Twenty-six.

Repeat them.

A, b, c, d, e, f, g, h, i, j, k, l, m, n, o, p, q, r, s, t, u, v, w, x, y, z.

What are the letters, when taken together in their regular order, as above, called?

The Alphabet.

How many of these letters can be sounded alone?

Five.

Which are they?

A, e, i, o, u.

What do we call these?

VOWELS.

What is a Vowel?

A **Vowel** is a letter that represents a complete sound.

Try to sound *b*. Can it be sounded alone? *

No; not unless a vowel is joined to it.

What are such letters as can not be sounded alone, called?

CONSONANTS.

What is a Consonant?

A **Consonant** is a letter that does not repre-sent a complete sound.

Are there any letters which are sometimes vowels, and at other times consonants?

Yes; *w* and *y*.

In the word *kindly*, how many distinct sounds are there?

Two; *kind* and *ly*.

What are these parts forming distinct sounds called?

SYLLABLES.

What is a Syllable?

A **Syllable** is one or more letters combined so as to form a distinct sound.

Divide the word *ramrod* into syllables. *Ram-rod.* Divide the word *minister* into syllables. *Min-is-ter.* Divide the word *sister* into syllables; *Henry; sickness; manful; manfully; elephant; wilderness; contemplate; circumstance; commiserate; Constantinople.*

You have said that *w* and *y* are sometimes vowels, and at other times consonants; when are they consonants?

When they begin a syllable.

When are *w* and *y* vowels?

When they do not begin a syllable.

Is *w* a vowel or a consonant in *wine?* in *wife?* in *new?* in *westerly?* in *Yorktown?* in *bow?* in *world?* in *William?* in *waterworks?* in *saw?* in *wave?*

Is *y* a vowel or a consonant in *youth?* in *Mary?* in *boy?* in *yesterday?* in *New York?* in *yawn?* in *syllable?*

How many and which of the letters are always vowels?

Five; *a, e, i, o, u.*

* The teacher will do well to make the pupil thoroughly understand the difference between the *name* of a letter and its *sound*, and to illustrate the point with examples.

How many and which of the letters are vowels, when they do not stand at the commencement of a word or syllable?

Two; *w* and *y.*

How many and which are always consonants?

Nineteen; *b, c, d, f, g, h, j, k, l, m, n, p, q, r, s, t, v, x, z.*

LESSON II.

WORDS.—PARTS OF SPEECH.—ARTICLES.

WHAT do you use, when you want to speak your thoughts?

WORDS.

What is a Word?

A **Word** is what is spoken or written as the sign of an idea; as, *book.*

How are words divided?

Into different classes, called PARTS OF SPEECH.

How many parts of speech are there, and what are they called?

Nine: viz, Article, Noun, Pronoun, Adjective, Verb, Adverb, Conjunction, Preposition, and Interjection.

What is the first part of speech?

The ARTICLE.

What is an Article?

An **Article** is a word placed before another word, to show whether it is used in a particular, or in a general, sense.

How many articles are there?

Two; *The,* and *An* or *A.*

When we say *the man,* what do we mean?

Some particular man.

When we say *a man,* do we refer to a *particular* man?

No; to *any* man.

What is *the* called, and why?

THE is called the Definite Article, because it defines or points out a particular object.

What is *an* or *a* called, and why?

AN or A is called the Indefinite Article, because it does not define or point out any particular object.

Are A and AN the same article?

Yes; they are different forms of the same article.

Where is *a* used?

A is used before a word commencing with a consonant, or a consonant sound; as, *a goat, a bench, a unit.*

What vowels standing at the commencement of a word, have a consonant sound?

U long (as in *unit*), and *eu,* when they stand at the commencement of a word, are pronounced as if the consonant *y* stood before them; thus, *unit, use, eulogy, Europe.*

Do you use *a* or *an,* then, before words commencing with *u* long and *eu?*

A ; because such words commence with a consonant sound; as, *a unit, a eulogy.*

Where is *an* used?

Before words commencing with a vowel, or with an *h* that is not sounded; as, *an enemy, an inkstand, an hour, an heir.*

Mention again before what words *a* is used.

Before what words is *an* used?

EXERCISE.*

The pupil must in no case attempt to write the Exercise until he is fully prepared to answer the questions that precede it.

---

* It is intended that all parts of this work headed EXERCISE should be written at home, and brought to the teacher for cor-

Insert the definite article before each of the following words:—

mouse,	lady,	tigers,	steamboat,	clock,
squirrels,	book,	cloak,	rhinoceros,	woman,
inkstand,	pencils,	boy,	elephant,	goose,
teachers,	thief,	girl,	balloons,	drama.

Insert the indefinite article before each of the following nouns, being careful to follow the directions given above for the use of *a* and *an:*—

hermit,	wilderness,	hurricane,	eulogy,
apple,	upstart,	alligator,	festival,
urchin,	wonder,	hundred,	husband,
hunter,	urn,	youngster,	Indian,
yeoman,	ewe,	waterman,	hyacinth.

LESSON III.

NOUNS.

WHAT is the second part of speech?

The Noun.

What is your name? What is the name of the state in which you live? What word means the same as *name?*

Noun.

What, then, may your name and that of your state be called?

Nouns.

---

rection. It will be well for him to underline such words as are misspelled or improperly used, and require the pupil to correct them himself.

What is a Noun?

A **Noun** is the name of any person, place, or thing; as, *James, Boston, bench.*

To show that you understand this, mention three nouns, the names of persons; three, the names of places; three, the names of things.

How many classes of nouns are there?

Two; Common and Proper.

What is a Common Noun?

A **Common Noun** is a name that distinguishes one class of things from another; as, *man, city, river.*

What is a Proper Noun?

A **Proper Noun** is a name that distinguishes one individual of a class from another; as *Byron, Brooklyn, Hudson.*

How do proper nouns always commence?

With a capital letter.

Is *chair* a proper or a common noun? *lion? George? Alps? Connecticut? factory? Wednesday? summer?*

EXERCISE.

Write out a list of the nouns in the following sentences, commencing the common nouns with small letters, and the proper nouns with capitals:—

1. George is going to Boston on Monday.

2. Many towns and villages are situated on the Mohawk.

3. Victoria is queen of England.

4. We like the city better than the country.

5. Grammar is an important study.

6. Bees make honey, and lay it up in hives.

Complete the following sentences by inserting

in place of the dash,* a noun, common or proper, as the sense may require :—

The Teacher, in correcting the exercises, will see that the punctuation of the book is followed. Rules on this subject will be furnished hereafter.

EXAMPLE. —— are ripe in summer.
Completed. *Blackberries* are ripe in summer.

7. —— is one of the United States of America.

8. In summer, the —— are unable to endure the heat of the ——, and retire into the ——.

9. The elephant is one of the largest of ——; he has a rough —— of a dark ——; his —— are small, but bright and penetrating;, he moves his —— like a fan, to drive away flies from his ——. With his trunk he raises food to his ——, and draws —— to quench his ——,When he is tamed, he obeys his ——, and at his —— will kneel to receive a ——. Elephants are said to live more than a hundred ——.

LESSON IV.

PRONOUNS.

WHEN I say, "*John learns his lesson,*" what does the word *his* stand for?

John's.

How would the sentence read, if we should use *John's* instead of *his?*

John learns John's lesson.

* NOTE. A dash is a short horizontal line (——).

What part of speech is *John's*, and why?

A noun; because it is the name of a person.

What is a word that stands instead of a noun, called?

A PRONOUN.

What is a Pronoun?

A **Pronoun** is a word used instead of a noun.

Why is a pronoun used instead of a noun?

Because it would not sound well to have the noun repeated too often.

Give an example.

John respects John's father, John's mother, and John's teacher.

How does this sentence read, when the pronoun is used instead of *John's?*

Name some of the principal pronouns.

I, my, mine, me, we, our, ours, us, thou, thy, thine, thee, you, your, yours, he, his, him, she, her, hers, it, its, they, their, theirs, them, who, which, that.

Mention the pronouns in the following sentences, and, as you name each, tell the noun for which it stands:—

1. James, who had studied hard, recited his lesson well.

2. Mary is a good girl, for she obeys her parents.

3. Be virtuous, and you will obtain your reward.

4. James and George have performed the task which I gave them.

What is a noun?

What is a pronoun?

Mention again some of the pronouns that are most in use.

EXERCISE.

Where a dash occurs, insert the proper pronoun.

EXAMPLE. This apple is mine, but—— will give it to ——.

Completed. This apple is mine, but *I* will give it to *you*.

1. William asked —— father to take —— into the country.

2. I love —— friends.

3. Julia has gone to —— dinner.

4. Where is —— hat? I hung —— on the nail.

5. Parents love —— children, and take care of ——.

6. John, where are —— going?

7. We gave the poor woman a penny, and she put —— into —— bag.

8. Here is a bird's nest —— I found in the woods. —— is made of straw and moss, —— the old birds find in the fields.

9. Jane and —— brother have gone to —— cousin's.

10. I will give you a handsome prize, if —— are a diligent boy and attend to —— duties.

11. The man —— is honest, will be respected by all —— acquaintances.

12. Washington, in —— youth, and throughout —— whole life, adhered strictly to the truth, and thus set an example which —— ought to follow.

13. If we think we never do wrong, —— deceive ourselves, for almost every moment —— are guilty of sin.

14. We ought to remember the favors which are conferred on —— by —— friends.

15. Nature is before us, and invites —— to contemplate the greatness and goodness of —— Creator.

16. Miss Pardoe, in —— book of Travels, gives —— many interesting particulars respecting the Turks, their habits, —— religion, and —— government. —— says that one of the most attractive features in —— charac- ter is the respect —— they entertain for the aged.

LESSON V.

ADJECTIVES.

WHAT is the fourth part of speech called?

The ADJECTIVE.

In the sentence, " *Be a good boy*," which word is a noun?

Why is it a noun?

Which word describes *boy*, or tells what kind of a boy is meant?

Good.

What is *good* called?

An Adjective.

What is an Adjective?

An **Adjective** is a word used to describe or limit a noun or pronoun; as, *a bad man, an active child, John is obedient.* In these sentences, *bad, active,* and *obedient* are adjectives.

What do adjectives sometimes express besides quality?

Number; as, *three men, the fourth row.* *Three* and *fourth* are adjectives.

What are adjectives that express number, called?

NUMERAL ADJECTIVES.

Mention three adjectives. Mention three numeral adjectives.

EXERCISE.

Complete the following sentences by inserting an adjective in place of each dash. No adjective must be repeated; find a new one in each case.

EXAMPLE. A —— cow. With an adjective inserted, a *fat* cow; or, a *lean* cow; or, a *small* cow; or, a *white* cow.

1. It is a —— day; the weather is ——.

2. Columbus was the —— man that crossed the —— ocean.

3. The whale is a —— animal; with his tail he often upsets boats, and destroys —— men.

4. In a garden we see many —— flowers; the —— rose, the —— violet, and the —— lily.

5. We live in a —— house, which has —— stories.

6. I saw a company of —— soldiers, well armed with —— rifles.

7. He has walked a —— distance, and is ——.

8. Be —— to your teachers, and —— to your parents.

9. He that is —— and —— when he is young, will be —— when he is old.

10. William has a —— dog, a —— kitten, and a —— horse.

11. I found some —— apples, and —— pears, in the orchard.

12. In the West Indies, they have very——weather and —— storms. The climate is considered —— for sick persons.

LESSON VI.

VERBS.

What is the fifth part of speech called?

The Verb.

In the sentence, "*Jane eats cake*," which word tells us what Jane does?

Eats.

In the sentence, "*Mary sleeps*," which word tells us the state Mary is in?

Sleeps.

What do we call *eats* and *sleeps?*

Verbs.

What is a Verb?

A **Verb** is a word that affirms an action or a state.

In the sentence, "*John is good*," what part of speech is *John*, and why? What is *is*, and why? What is *good*, and why?

Mention in order the verbs in the following sentences:—

Oxen are large and strong animals; they submit to the yoke, plough the fields, and draw heavy carts. The farmer fattens them, kills them for food, and takes them to market.

EXERCISE.

Where a dash occurs, insert a verb that will complete the sense.

EXAMPLE. The oak —— a firm root, and —— the winter storm.

Completed. The oak *has* a firm root, and *resists* the winter storm.

1. The horse —— a noble and useful animal. He can —— or ——, and at the same time —— a man on his back, or —— a wagon behind him.

2. Wandering Arabs —— in the desert. They —— themselves near the springs, and —— travellers when they stop to —— water.

3. A farmer —— a snake, almost frozen to death, under a hedge; moved with compassion, he ——it up, —— it to his house, and —— it near the fire. No sooner did the heat —— to revive it, than the snake —— upon his wife, —— one of his children, and —— the whole family into terror and confusion. "Ungrate-

ful wretch!" —— the farmer; "I find it —— useless
to —— favors on the undeserving." With these words
he —— a hatchet, and —— the snake into pieces.

4. In autumn, the farmer —— his harvest, and ——
it away in barns. The leaves —— from the trees, and
the wind —— through the branches.

5. Whatever you —— to do, —— it quickly; never
—— till to-morrow what —— to-day.

6. Let us —— early, to see the sun ——.

7. Cows —— milk, which —— into butter and cheese.

8. He —— to the concert, to —— Jenny Lind sing.

——•——

LESSON VII.

ADVERBS.

WHAT is the sixth part of speech called?

The ADVERB.

What is the meaning of the word *adverb?*

Joined to a verb.

Why are adverbs joined to verbs?

To modify them.

In the sentence, " *George struggled hard,*" what word tells
how he struggled?

Hard.

Then *hard* is joined to, or modifies, what word?

The verb *struggled.*

What part of speech, then, is *hard?*

An adverb.

Are adverbs ever joined to any other words besides verbs?

Yes; adverbs modify verbs, adjectives, and
other adverbs.

In the sentence, " *George struggled very hard,*" what word tells
how hard George struggled?

Very.

Then *very* is joined to *hard;* what part of speech is *hard?*

An adverb.

Then since *very* is joined to the adverb *hard*, what part of speech is it?

An adverb.

In the sentence, "*John is very obedient*," to what word is *very* joined?

To the adjective *obedient*.

What part of speech is it, then?

An adverb.

What is an Adverb?

An **Adverb** is a word used to modify a verb, an adjective, or another verb.

Select the adverbs in the following sentences, and tell what words they modify :—

1. John walks gracefully.

2. He studies very hard, and stands well in his class.

3. I like him very much.

Mention some of the principal classes of adverbs.

1. Adverbs of manner, which end for the most part in *ly;* as, swiftly, boldly, quickly, slowly, handsomely, &c.

2. Adverbs of time; as, now, then, yesterday, to-day, to-morrow, immediately, often, always, never, ever, again, soon, seldom, hitherto, &c.

3. Adverbs of place; as, here, there, hither, thither, whither, hence, thence, where, and its compounds nowhere, elsewhere, everywhere, &c.

4. Adverbs of quantity; as, much, little, enough, &c.

5. Adverbs of degree; as, very, almost, nearly, &c.

What other words express manner, and are therefore liable to be confounded with adverbs of manner?

Adjectives.

What is the difference between them?

An adjective is used to describe a noun; an

adverb, to describe or modify a verb, an adjective, or another adverb.

How can you tell them apart?

When a word expressing manner is joined to a noun or pronoun, it is an adjective; when it is joined to a verb, adjective, or adverb, it is an adverb.

EXERCISE.

Make a list, in order, of the adjectives that occur in the following sentences. Make a separate list of the adverbs, in order:—

1. I will assist you most cheerfully, if you will be careful and attenti e.

2. Those who evirtuous may not always be happy here, but they will certainly receive their reward hereafter.

3. Large armies generally march slowly.

4. He who forms conclusions too quickly, often forms them incorrectly.

5. If you are attentive, you will learn grammar very fast.

6. I have heard better singing to-day than I ever heard before.

7. He who tries hard, seldom fails to succeed.

8. Quicksilver is a very valuable metal; it has hitherto been imported chiefly from Spain, Germany, and Peru.

9. The Portuguese were once the most enterprising navigators of Europe; they founded colonies in many parts of the world, before totally unknown.

10. The Bedouin Arabs are, for the most part, small, meagre, and tawny.

11. The early hours of sleep are the most sweet and refreshing.

LESSON VIII.

EXERCISE ON ADVERBS.

WHAT is an adverb ? *

What are the principal classes of adverbs ?

Mention three adverbs of manner; three of time; three of place; three of quantity; three of degree.

What is the difference between an adjective and an adverb ?

EXERCISE.

Where a dash occurs, insert an adverb that will complete the sense.

EXAMPLE. I walked ——.

Completed. I walked *briskly.*

1. Mary sings ——, and dances ——.

2. The house is —— tall, and is —— built.

3. We are —— going to the grave.

4. I saw him ——; he was running —— down Broadway.

5. Listen ——, and you will —— be able to un-derstand the subject.

6. Cæsar —— started in pursuit; he —— overtook the enemy, —— led on the attack in person, and gained a complete victory.

7. Time past —— returns; improve the moments, therefore, as —— as you can.

8. The horse trotted ——. John ate ——.

9. The lion roars ——. The kitten plays ——.

---

* *Note to the Pupil.* When a question is repeated, and you have forgotten the answer, look back and find it, in order that you may give it in the precise words of the book.

10. The rain began to fall —, and they were ——
wet.

11. The poor dog was —— hurt.

12. This room will hold twenty persons very ——.

13. He —— gave the poor woman his purse.

14. When are you going? ——. (Insert an adverb
as an answer.)

15. Do you see him? Yes; he is ——.

———+———

LESSON IX.

CONJUNCTIONS.

WHAT is the seventh part of speech called?

The CONJUNCTION.

When I say, "*Mary learns her lessons,*" what is the expression
called?

A SENTENCE.

What is a Sentence?

A **Sentence** is such an assemblage of words as
makes complete sense.

Would "*Mary to the fair*" be a sentence?

No; because it would not make complete sense.

Make a complete sentence of it.

"*Mary has gone to the fair.*"

In the sentence, "*James got up early, and went to market,*" how
many parts are there, and what are they?

Two; "*James got up early*" is one, "*went to
market*" is the other.

What are such parts of a sentence called?

Clauses.

What word connects the two clauses in the above sentence?

And.

What does the word *conjunction* mean?

A connecting together.

What, then, may *and*, and all such words as connect clauses, be called?

Conjunctions.

Do conjunctions ever connect any thing else besides clauses?

Yes; conjunctions connect words also.

Give me a sentence in which there is a conjunction connecting words.

" *Mary turned and wept;* " here the conjunction *and* connects the verbs *turned* and *wept.*

Give me another.

George and Henry have gone to Boston; " here the conjunction *and* connects the nouns *George* and *Henry.*

Now tell me, what is a Conjunction?

A **Conjunction** is a word used to connect other words and clauses.

Mention some of the principal Conjunctions.

And, because, if, that, or, nor, either, neither, but, lest, notwithstanding, therefore, though, unless, than, as.

What is a sentence?

What is a clause?

What is a conjunction?

EXERCISE.

Where a dash occurs, insert a conjunction that will complete the sense.

EXAMPLE. He went to the ball, —— he was ordered to remain.

Completed. He went to the ball, *although* he was ordered to remain.

1. Either you must go, —— I. John —— Mary are here.

2. Neither the wagon —— the carriage has arrived.

3. We will not go a fishing, —— it rains.

4. Hannibal took an oath —— he would conquer the Romans.

5. He did not get a premium, —— he did not deserve it.

6. Mary has excellent parents, —— she is a bad girl.

7. Do not buy the book —— you can get it for a shilling.

8. I like to see a hard shower, —— I never walk out in one.

9. My father —— mother are going to Boston to-morrow, —— it be clear.

10. Let those who stand, beware —— they fall.

11. The happy often forget —— others are miserable.

12. General Taylor defeated the Mexicans, —— his army was much smaller —— theirs.

13. None will deny —— the hawk flies more swiftly —— the pigeon.

14. —— you do your duty, you will not be blamed.

15. I saw my cousin —— I was turning the corner.

LESSON X.

PREPOSITIONS.

WHAT is the eighth part of speech called?

The PREPOSITION.

In the sentence, "*William walked to Albany*," what word shows the relation between *William's walking* and *Albany?*

To,

How is this word *to* placed ?

Before the noun *Albany.*

What does the word *preposition* mean ?

A *placing before.*

What, then, may we call *to*, and all similar words ?

Prepositions.

What is a Preposition ?

A **Preposition** is a word placed before a noun or pronoun, to show the relation between it and some other word or words in the sentence.

Mention the principal prepositions.*

Among,	behind,	for,	through,
around,	below,	from,	throughout,
about,	beneath,	in,	to,
above,	beside,	into,	toward,
across,	between,	instead of,	up,
according to,	beyond,	near,	upon,
after,	by,	of,	under,
against,	concerning,	on,	unto,
amidst,	down,	out of,	with,
at,	during,	over,	within,
before,	except,	respecting,	without.

EXERCISE.

Wherever a dash occurs, insert a preposition that will complete the sense.

EXAMPLE. Nothing can be accomplished —— an effort.

Completed. Nothing can be accomplished *without* an effort.

1. In Greenland, the people live —— wretched huts.

* It will be well to commit this list to memory.

2. A steamboat runs —— Providence —— New York.

3. —— the summer, the cattle love to lie —— shady trees.

4. The camel has a hump —— his back.

5. —— patience and perseverance you may attain the highest station —— society.

6. He gave the book —— me, and I placed it —— the table.

7. You must do sums —— the rule.

8. It is dark —— sunset.

9. She lives —— Piermont, twenty-five miles —— New York.

10. A large rock hangs —— the path.

11. The sailor likes to get —— port.

12. Always keep virtue and duty —— your eyes.

13. I live —— my father.

14. A farmer was bitten —— a snake, while he was standing —— the weeds.

15. The ferry-boat will take us —— the river.

LESSON XI.

INTERJECTIONS.

WHAT is the ninth and last part of speech?

The INTERJECTION.

In the sentence, "*Alas! I am undone,*" what word is thrown in to express the sorrow of the speaker?

Alas!

What does the word *interjection* mean?

A throwing in.

What, then, may *alas!* and similar words be called?

Interjections.

What is an Interjection?

An **Interjection** is a word used to express some sudden feeling of the speaker.

What are the principal feelings which are expressed by interjections?

Sorrow, triumph, disgust, wonder; there are also interjections of calling, of attention, of saluting, of taking leave.

Mention the principal interjections of sorrow.

Oh! ah! alas! alack!

Mention those expressing triumph.

Hurrah! huzza! bravo! aha!

Mention those expressing disgust.

Fy! fudge! pshaw! tush! away! begone!

Mention those expressing wonder.

Indeed! strange! what!

Mention those of calling.

Hallo! ho!

Mention those of attention.

Behold! lo! hark! listen! see! hush! hist!

Mention those of saluting.

O! (*O* is always used with a pronoun, or the name of an object addressed; as, *O thou! O James!*) welcome! hail!

Mention those of taking leave.

Adieu! farewell! good b'ye!

What mark is that (!) which you see placed after each of the above interjections?

An Exclamation-point.

When you write an interjection, what must you place after it? An exclamation-point.

In the exercise that follows, how will you know which of the above interjections to insert in place of the dash?

I will read the whole sentence, and put in an interjection that is appropriate. Thus, if the sentence express *sorrow*, I will insert an interjection of *sorrow;* if *wonder*, I will insert one of *wonder*, &c.

EXERCISE.

Where a dash occurs, insert a suitable interjection.

EXAMPLE. ——! the victory is ours!

Completed. Hurrah! the victory is ours!

1. ——! I am surprised at this.

2. My house is on fire; ——! I am undone.

3. ——! what strange figure is this that is approaching?

4. ——! my friend; I am glad to see you.

5. ——! the cannon are booming; the battle has begun.

6. ——! dishonest wretch; I despise thee!

7. ——! our friend has conquered.

8. ——! stranger; will you tell a traveller where he is?

9. ——! no one can tell how much the poor suffer.

10. ——! is it thus you behave?

11. I hope you may have a pleasant journey. ——!

12. ——! what noise was that?

13. ——! poor fellow! I am sorry for him.

14. ——! John, where are you going?

15. Who is that? ——! he is descending the hill.

16. ——! is it really so? Impossible!

17. ——! thou blessed sun, that spreadest gladness over the earth.

18. ——! I am at the head of my class.

LESSON XII.

A REVIEW.

[The pupil has answered all the questions given below, as they occurred in the preceding lessons; but as he may have forgotten some of them, he must look back for the answers, and learn them carefully.]

WHAT is a letter?

What is a vowel? Name the vowels.

What is a consonant? Name the consonants.

What two letters are sometimes vowels, and at other times consonants?

When are they vowels, and when consonants?

What is a syllable?

What is a word?

How many parts of speech are there? Mention them.

What is an article? Mention the articles. Which of these is the indefinite article, and which the definite?

What is a noun? Give an example.

How many kinds of nouns are there? What is a proper noun? What is a common noun? Give examples.

What is a pronoun? Mention some of the principal pronouns.

What is an adjective? Give an example.

What is a verb? Give an example.

What is an adverb? Give an example. Mention the different kinds of adverbs, and give an example of each.

What is the difference between adjectives and adverbs?

What is a sentence?

What are distinct parts of sentences called?

What is a conjunction? Mention some of the principal conjunctions.

What is a preposition? Mention some of the principal prepositions.

What is an interjection? What are the principal classes of interjections? Mention one of each class.

What mark is placed after an interjection?

LESSON XIII.

MISCELLANEOUS EXERCISE.

In this lesson and the next, the pupil, wherever a dash occurs, must insert whatever part of speech is required to complete the sense. Follow the spelling and punctuation of the book.

MARTINS.

MARTINS —— a kind of swallows. They feed —— flies, ——, and other insects, and skim swiftly through —— air, in pursuit of their prey. In the morning —— are up by daybreak, and twitter about your window, while —— are asleep —— bed. They are —— harmless, and, as people do not molest them, they —— build their —— in towns —— villages. They are small birds, but —— a great deal. I will —— a couple of stories, illustrating their sagacity.

A pair of martins, who —— their nest in —— porch, had some young ones; and —— happened that one of them, in —— to climb —— the side, fell out, and striking —— the stones, was —— killed. The old ——, seeing this accident, went and —— —— strong pieces of straw, and fastened them —— m   all around the ——, in order to keep the —— from meaning a similar ——.

Here is another —— about them. While a martin was absent from his nest, one day, a —— cock-sparrow took possession —— it; —— when the owner —— and —— to enter, he put out —— bill, and commenced pecking at him. The martin, not —— pleased with this invasion of his ——, flew away, and —— a number of his companions. They all came —— the nest, with bits of clay in their ——, with which —— plastered up the —— to the nest; so —— the sparrow, unable to —— food and air, —— died.

2*

LESSON XIV.

EXERCISE.

THE DUKE AND THE GALLEY-SLAVES.

THE King of Spain once gave —— to —— Duke of Ossuna to release such of the galley-slaves as —— might think proper. The Duke, as he —— among the slaves who were —— at the oars, asked them in succession of what crime they had ——guilty. They all protested innocence, and —— him that they had been unjustly One attributed his condemnation to the —— of an enemy, another to the —— of his judge. At last, however, he —— one who admitted that, to save his —— from starving, he had robbed a man of ——, on —— highway. The Duke, —— he heard this, gave him a stroke —— the back —— his hand, and said, " Get you gone, you rogue, from the —— of honest men." So —— who confessed——fault was released, while the ——, for their want of ——, were compelled to —— at their labors.

Thus we see —— we are not likely to lose any thing by a —— admission of —— faults.

———◆———

LESSON XV.

THE SUBJECT.

WHEN I say, " *Charles walks*," who is it that I speak about ?
Charles.

In the sentence, " *The oak has been cut down*," what is it that I speak about ?

The *oak*.

What do we call *Charles*, *oak*, and all words respecting which an action or state is affirmed?

SUBJECTS.

What is the Subject of a verb?

The **Subject** of a verb is that respecting which the action or state expressed by the verb is affirmed.

How may you always find the subject of a verb?

Put the word *who* or *what* before the verb, and the answer to the question will be the subject.

Give an example. In the sentence, "*John went to market*," what is the subject?

Put *who* before the verb, and the answer to the question will be the subject. Thus, "*Who* went to market?" Answer, *John*. *John* is the subject.

In the sentence, "*Virtue is a source of happiness*," find the subject in the same manner as above.

Put *what* before the verb; "*What* is a source of happiness?" Answer, *Virtue*. *Virtue* is the subject.

In the same manner select the subjects in the following sentences:—

Bees make honey. Virginia is a large state.

Quarrels are unpleasant. Charles was late at school.

The flute makes fine music. We are tired of walking.

The machine was invented in England. You are wrong.

Gratitude is a noble feeling. Science enlarges the mind.

They are very sick. We were disappointed.

In the last two sentences, what are the subjects?

They and *we*.

What part of speech are *they* and *we?*

Pronouns.

May pronouns, then, be the subjects of a verb?

They may.

In the sentence, " *To steal is base*," find the subject as above.

Put *what* before the verb: " *What* is base ? " Answer, *to steal.* *To steal* is the subject.

What part of speech is *steal ?*

A verb, because it expresses action.

When a verb has *to* before it, we say that it is in the *infinitive mood;* may a verb in the infinitive mood, then, be the subject of another verb ?

It may.

What mood is a verb in, when it has *to* before it ?

A verb is in the infinitive mood, when it has *to* before it.

How may we know when a verb is in the infinitive mood ?

By seeing whether it has *to* before it.

Is *to play* in the infinitive mood ? *to jump ?* *to walk ?* Mention six more verbs in the infinitive mood.

May a verb in the infinitive mood be the subject of another verb ?

It may.

Give me several examples, and mention the subject.

To lie is dishonorable : here, *to lie* is the subject. *To travel is pleasant :* *to travel* is the subject.

Make three short sentences of your own, like the above, in which a verb in the infinitive mood will be the subject of another verb, and mention the subject in each sentence.

In the sentence, " *Whether we shall go to Boston is uncertain*," find the subject in the manner described above.

Put *what* before the verb : " *What* is uncertain ? " Answer, *whether we shall go to Boston.* These words, therefore, *whether we shall go to Boston,* are the subject.

These words form part of a sentence; may, then, part of a sentence be the subject of a verb ?

It may.

Find, as above, the subjects in the following sentences :—

1. To fall from the top of a church-steeple, is certain death.

2. For a weak nation to provoke a strong one, is bad policy.

3. That even the best men commit sin, is proved by daily experience.

Now, let us see, what have we found that a verb may have for its subject?

A verb may have for its subject,

I. A noun; as, *John walks.*

II. A pronoun; as, *They have gone.*

III. A verb in the infinitive mood; as, *To dig is hard work.*

IV. Part of a sentence; as, *Doing one's duty secures happiness.*

Select the subject in each of the sentences just given as examples.

EXERCISE.

Select and write out the subject in each of the following sentences; if you are in doubt, put *who* or *what* before the verb, as directed above:—

EXAMPLE. Working in quicksilver mines is very injurious to the health.

Subject. Working in quicksilver mines.

1. We should improve our time.
2. Digging potatoes is hard work.
3. To reveal a friend's secrets is dishonorable.
4. Cicero was a celebrated orator.
5. Wealth does not always procure esteem.
6. Temperance and exercise preserve health.
7. Time and tide wait for no man.
8. For an ignorant person to profess to teach philosophy, only exposes him to ridicule.

9. Whether it will rain, is uncertain.

10. John and I will start in the morning.

11. Where are the women going?

12. To be wise in his own eyes, is the mark of a fool.

LESSON XVI.

EXERCISE.

WHERE a dash occurs, insert a subject; either a noun, a pronoun, a verb in the infinitive mood, or part of a sentence, as may be required to complete the sense.

EXAMPLE. —— and —— lead to wealth.

Completed. *Industry* and *frugality* lead to wealth.

1. —— and —— gnaw holes in the floor.

2. ——, ——, and ——, are used for drawing loads.

3. ——* is dishonorable.

4. —— am going to school.

5. —— is a useful study.

6. Has the —— arrived?

7. —— attends carefully to his lessons.

8. Have —— written your exercise?

9. —— and —— are made from milk.

10. ——* is a proof of dishonesty.

11. ——* is the practice of a bad boy.

12. ——* is unpleasant work.

13. ——* is the business of the baker.

14. —— marched by with a fine band of music.

* Here the pupil must insert a verb in the infinitive mood or part of a sentence.

LESSON XVII.

THE OBJECT.—TRANSITIVE AND INTRANSITIVE VERBS.

In the sentence, " *Charles killed a fly*," what word expresses the object on which the action is exerted?

The word *fly*.

What do we call *fly*, in this sentence?

Fly is the OBJECT of the verb *killed*.

In the sentence, " *Children love milk*," what is the object of the verb *love?*

Milk.

What is the Object of a verb?

The **Object** of a verb is that on which the action expressed by the verb is exerted.

What is the object in each of the following sentences?

Bees make honey.   Birds build nests.

Mary kindled the fire.   I have broken my knife.

My mother loves me.   John's father scolded him.

In the last two sentences what are the objects?

Me and *him*.

What part of speech are *me* and *him?*

Pronouns.

May a pronoun, then, be the object of a verb?

It may.

In the sentence, " *John sleeps*," is there any object?

There is not.

Does the verb *sleep* admit an object after it?

It does not.

Into how many classes, then, may verbs be divided?

Into two classes :—

I. TRANSITIVE verbs, which express an act that may be done to an object.

II. INTRANSITIVE verbs, which do not express an
act that may be done to an objectet.

Are verbs that express simply *a state of being* transitive or intransitive?

Verbs that express a state of being are intransitive.

Why?

Because they do not express any action at all.

Is *strike* transitive or intransitive, and why?

Strike is a transitive verb, because it admits an
object after it. Thus we may say, " I strike a
man; " in this sentence, *man* would be the object,
and hence we find that *strike* is transitive.

Is *live* a transitive or an intransitive verb?

Live is an intransitive verb, because it expresses
simply a state of being, and does not admit an object after it.

Is *sleep* transitive or intransitive? *jump? hurt? eat? dream?
love? see? be? walk? run?*

May any other part of speech besides a verb have an object?

Yes; a preposition may have an object.

In the sentence, " *John is lying on the grass,*" what is the object of the preposition *on?*

Grass.

Make three short sentences similar to the one last given, in
which there will be a preposition and its object.

How may you always find the object of a verb or preposition?

By putting *what* or *whom* after it; the answer
to the question will be the object.

Give me an example. Tell me the object of the verb and
preposition in this sentence, " *The butcher killed a pig with a
knife.*"

Put *what* after the verb : " The butcher killed
what? " Answer, a *pig; pig* is the object of the

verb *killed.* Put *what* after the preposition :
" With *what ?* " Answer, a *knife ; knife* is the
object of the preposition *with.*

Complete the following sentences by inserting
an object where a dash occurs ; either a noun or
pronoun, as the sense may require :—

1. In Egypt the Nile overflows the ——, and renders the —— fertile.

2. Boys can buy —— with their money.

3. I have found in the street a —— and a ——.

4. A man, by honesty and ——, will always gain the
—— of his companions.

5. Henry's father bought him a —— for a Christmas ——.

6. When danger is nigh, a hen gathers her ——
under her ——.

7. The fisherman is preparing to go to—— in a ——.

8. In building houses, they use——, ——, and——.

9. The mice have gnawed —— in this old ——.

10. The American Indians are very skilful with the
bow and arrow ; they can hit a very small —— at a
great ——. With these weapons they often kill ——,
——, and other wild ——.

11. With your spare —— purchase books ; read
——, profit by ——, and take good care of ——.

12. My brother loves me, and I love ——.

13. After we die, the grave will contain our —— ;
but our friends will remember ——, and shed —— on
account of our departure.

14. Birds gather —— for their young, and teach
—— how to fly.

15. The milk of the cow furnishes us —— and ——.

16. In church we see many ——, but should listen to the ——.

LESSON XVIII.

PERSONAL, RELATIVE, INTERROGATIVE, AND ADJECTIVE PRONOUNS.*

WHAT is a pronoun? (See Lesson IV., if you forget.)

How many different classes of pronouns are there, and what are their names?

There are four classes of pronouns; Personal, Relative, Interrogative, and Adjective.

In the sentence, "*I am tired,*" for what does the pronoun *I* stand?

For the name of the person speaking.

What kind of a pronoun is *I?*

A PERSONAL pronoun.

What is a Personal Pronoun?

A **Personal Pronoun** is a word, which, being used in a sentence without the noun for which it stands, merely represents it, without introducing any other idea respecting it.

Mention the personal pronouns.

The personal pronouns are as follows: *I, my, mine, me, we, our, ours, us, thou, thy, thine, thee, you, your, yours, he, his, him, she, her, hers, it, its, they, their, theirs, them.*

In the sentence, "*The Romans, who were victorious, lost only*

* *Note.* No allusion is made in this lesson to the Compound Personal Pronouns, *myself, thyself,* &c., or the Compound Relatives, *whoever, whosoever, whichever,* &c., because a knowledge of them does not seem to be essential to the subject, and because the author feared that a consideration of these subdivisions might embarrass the pupil.

fifty men," to what word does the pronoun *who* relate; or, in other words, who are said to have been victorious?

Romans.

Then, since the pronoun *who* relates to *Romans,* what kind of a pronoun shall we call it?

A RELATIVE pronoun.

What is a Relative Pronoun?

A **Relative Pronoun** is a word that relates to a noun or pronoun before it.

What is this noun or pronoun going before, to which the relative relates, called?

The Antecedent.

In the sentence, " *The boy who is idle will be unhappy,*" what is the relative, and what its antecedent?

Who is the relative, and *boy* is its antecedent.

Mention the relative pronouns.

The relative pronouns are *who, whose, whom, which, that.*

Is *who* always a relative pronoun?

No ; sometimes it does not relate to an antecedent, but is used to ask a question; as, " *Who is there ?* "

What kind of a pronoun is it then called?

An INTERROGATIVE pronoun.

What is an Interrogative Pronoun?

An **Interrogative Pronoun** is one that is used to ask a question.

Mention the interrogative pronouns.

The interrogative pronouns are *who, whose, whom, which,* and *what.*

What mark always follows a sentence that contains an interrogative pronoun?

The Interrogation-point (?), which ought to be placed after every question.

How, then, can you tell when *who* is a relative pronoun, and when an interrogative?

By looking at the end of the sentence; if the interrogation-point is there, it is for the most part an interrogative pronoun; if not, it is a relative.

What are Adjective Pronouns?

Adjective Pronouns are words that are sometimes used instead of nouns, but are more frequently followed by their nouns, which they limit, or qualify, after the manner of adjectives.

Give one or two sentences containing adjective pronouns.

" Hand me *that* book." " I have *some* apples." " Have you *any* paper? " *That, some,* and *any,* are adjective pronouns.

Mention some of the principal adjective pronouns.

This, that, these, those, some, no, none, any, all, each, every, either, neither.

Give examples of adjective pronouns used instead of nouns.

" *That* was unexpected." " *All* were pleased, and *some* delighted.

EXERCISE.

Make lists of the personal, relative, interrogative, and adjective pronouns, in order, as they occur in the following sentences. The pupil will do well to make his lists according to the following

EXAMPLE. Jane, I told you to hand me that book which is lying on the table, but you have not done it. What is the reason?

Lists.	*Personal.*	*Relative.*	*Interrogative.*	*Adjective.*
	I, you, me, you, it.	Which.	What.	That.

1. You say that* I am charged with a great crime. Who are my accusers? Let them stand forth, that I may see the authors of this base slander.

2. If every man would do his duty, none would have any cause for complaint.

3. Can we stand patiently by, and see our property torn from us? No; each generous emotion of our hearts forbids it. Let this tyrant tremble, and all his satellites beware!

4. The men whom I saw, had each a musket.

5. Wherever she went, every one seemed disposed to do her honor.

6. Look on this picture and on that.

———◆———

LESSON XIX.

RELATIVE PRONOUN AND RELATIVE CLAUSE.

What is a Relative Pronoun?

A Relative Pronoun is one that relates to a noun or pronoun going before, called the antecedent.

What is the Antecedent?

The Antecedent is the noun or pronoun before the relative to which it relates.

---

* *Note.* The word *that* is sometimes a conjunction, sometimes a relative, and at other times an adjective pronoun; the pupil must decide which it is by the relation that it bears to other words in the sentence. In this sentence, *that* is not a relative, for it does not relate to any antecedent; it is not an adjective pronoun, for it is not joined to, or used for, any noun; but it is a conjunction, for it connects clauses.

In the sentence, "*He that does right will be rewarded*," what is the relative, and what the antecedent?

That is the relative, and *he* is the antecedent.

What service does the relative perform in a sentence?

The relative is used to introduce a clause, for the purpose of limiting, explaining, or adding something further to what is said.

What is a clause thus introduced by a relative called?

A RELATIVE CLAUSE.

What is the relative clause in the sentence, "*He that does right will be rewarded*"?

That does right is the relative clause, because it is introduced by the relative *that*.

Select the relative, the antecedent, and the relative clause, in the following sentences :—

1. The friends that we gain in childhood, often forget us in old age.

2. The wind, which had been shifting all day from point to point, now began to blow steadily from the south.

3. Those who are the most industrious, are the most happy.

4. James, whose work was the best, received the premium.

5. I have seen the man that lives in the cave.

EXERCISE.

The sentences given in this exercise contain a relative and its antecedent; the pupil must complete the relative clause by inserting the necessary words. Before attempting to complete the clause, read the whole sentence, and then think of something that will be appropriate.

EXAMPLE. The study that —— is History.

Completed. The study that *I like best* is History.

Or, The study that *I dislike most* is History.

Or, The study that *I find most difficult* is History.

Each sentence may be completed in a variety of ways.

1. I have broken my watch, which ——.

2. The tree that ——, was blown down last night.

3. My father, who ——, is now well.

4. Those who —— will be happy in this world, and still happier in the next.

5. Horses are very useful to those who ——.

6. In every school there are boys who ——.

7. Thomas found the knife which ——.

8. There is a boy whose ——.

9. Mary is the most diligent girl that ——.

10. The good boy will apply himself vigorously to the lessons which ——.

11. The carriage which —— has been mended.

12. Columbus was the first man that ——.

13. The butterflies which ——, will all perish in winter.

14. The dog that —— has run away.

LESSON XX.

PARTICIPLES.—PARTICIPIAL CLAUSES.

IN the sentence, "*I saw John feeding his chickens,*" what word implies action, and at the same time qualifies John?

Feeding.

Which part of speech implies action, and which qualifies nouns?

The *verb* implies action, and the *adjective* qualifies nouns.

The word *feeding*, then, partakes of the nature of what two parts of speech?

The verb and the adjective.

What name is given to *feeding*, and similar words?

PARTICIPLES.

What is a Participle?

A **Participle** is a word that describes a noun or pronoun, by assigning to it a certain action or state.

Does the participle form a distinct part of speech?

No; participles are classed as parts of verbs.

How many participles has every transitive verb?

Five.

Mention the five participles of the verb *love*.

Loving, loved, having loved, being loved, having been loved.

How many participles has every intransitive verb?

Two.

Mention the two participles of the intransitive verb *walk*.

Walking, having walked.

Give me two or three sentences containing participles, and select the participle in each.

James, while *walking* by the shore, saw a large bass *attacked* by a shark.

Having been deceived once, I never trusted him again.

He died, *loved* and *respected* by all that knew him.

In the last sentence, what clause is introduced by the participles *loved* and *respected?*

" *Loved and respected by all that knew him.*"

What is a clause introduced by, or containing, a participle, called?

A PARTICIPIAL CLAUSE.

Select the participial clause in each of the three sentences given above.

Complete the following sentences by inserting a participle in place of the dash :—

EXAMPLE. The day —— fair, we started on our journey.

Completed. The day *being* fair, we started on our journey.

1. Moses, —— his lessons, recited them well.

2. We saw a boy —— in the river.

3. Dinner ——, the party sat down.

4. The carriage having been broken, Robert has taken it to the blacksmith's, to get it ——.

5. My dog —— sick, I could not go a hunting.

6. I have just seen a man killed by —— from the top of a house.

7. My friend, while —— out on horseback, was thrown and seriously injured.

8. I saw the American flag —— from the City Hall.

9. You may often see bad boys —— in the street.

10. Our house ——, we are about to move into it.

11. The merchant spends his time in —— and —— goods.

12. Gas is useful for —— streets and houses.

13. Oxen are used for —— wagons.

14. Ships, while —— on the ocean, often encounter violent storms.

15. The weather is cold, and we must have a fire ——.

16. From this eminence —— my eyes upon the vast plain that lay —— before me, I saw a herd of buffaloes —— amid the long prairie-grass, and a group of wild horses —— away in the far distance.

17. He was a bad man, and died, —— and —— by all that knew him.

3

LESSON XXI.

A REVIEW.

[For the answers to the following questions, see Lessons XV., XVII., XVIII., XIX., and XX.]

WHAT is the subject of a verb?

How may you find the subject of a verb?

What may a verb have for its subject?

What is the object of a verb?

What are transitive verbs?   What are intransitive verbs?

What other part of speech, besides transitive verbs, may have an object?

How may you find the object of a verb or preposition?

What is a pronoun?

Name the four classes of pronouns.

What is a personal pronoun?   Mention the personal pronouns.

What is a relative pronoun?   Mention the relative pronouns.

What is an interrogative pronoun?   Mention the interrogative pronouns.

What is an adjective pronoun?   Mention some of the principal adjective pronouns.

What is a relative clause?

What is the antecedent of a relative pronoun?

What is a participle?

How many participles has a transitive verb?   How many has an intransitive verb?

Mention the participles of the verb *ask*.   Mention those of the verb *dream*.

What is a participial clause?

EXERCISE.

Where the dash occurs, put in one or more words, as may be required to complete the sense.

THE TAME BEAR.

Hans Christian Andersen, the Danish writer, tells us the following —— story of a tame bear, which broke

loose while the man —— exhibiting him was —— dinner. He made his way to —— public house, ——, and
went straight —— where there were three children, the
eldest —— whom was no more than six or eight ——
old. "The door sprang open, and in walked ——.
The children were much frightened ——, and crept
—— corners. The bear followed ——, and rubbed
them with —— nose, but he did not ——. When the
children ——, they thought it was a big dog, and they
patted, ——, and ——. The eldest boy now —— his
drum, and began to —— loud noise. No sooner did
the bear ——, than he raised himself on —— and began to dance. This was charming.

The boys had been playing at soldiers before ——,
and now each —— his gun and ——. They gave the
bear a gun, too, and he —— like a regular militia-man.
Then they marched; what a fine comrade ——!

Presently, however, the door —— again. It was
the children's mother. You should have seen her; her
face was white as ——, and she trembled with fear
when she ——. Then the smallest —— ran up to her,
and shouted 'Mamma, mamma, we have had such ——,
playing soldier!'"

——•——

LESSON XXII.

SENTENCES, PHRASES, CLAUSES, APPOSITION.

WHAT is a Sentence?

A Sentence is such an assemblage of words as
makes complete sense.

How many kinds of sentences are there, and what are they?

Four kinds; Declarative, Imperative, Interrogative, and Exclamatory.

What is a Declarative Sentence?

A **Declarative Sentence** is one in which something is declared; as, " It rains."

What is an Imperative Sentence?

An **Imperative Sentence** is one in which permission is given, or a command, an exhortation, or an entreaty uttered; as, " Let it rain."

What is an Interrogative Sentence?

An **Interrogative Sentence** is one in which a question is asked; as, " Does it rain?"

What is an Exclamatory Sentence?

An **Exclamatory Sentence** is one that contains an exclamation; as, " How it rains!"

Make two declarative sentences; two imperative; two interrogative; two exclamatory.

What is a Phrase? *

A **Phrase** is a combination of words which *separately* have no connection, either in construction or sense, with other words in the sentence, but which, *when taken together*, convey a single idea, and may be construed as a single word. Thus: " James, in short, has become a hermit,"—in this sentence, *in short* is a phrase.

What is a Clause?

A **Clause** is a combination of words which *separately* may or may not be connected in construction with other words in the sentence: if so connected, they assert some additional circumstance respecting

---

* *Note to the Teacher.* It seems impossible to define the terms *phrase* and *clause* without employing a great many words. The teacher must exercise his discretion as to whether these definitions shall be committed to memory, or not. The pupil must, however, understand them perfectly, so as to be able to select phrases and clauses as they occur in sentences.

the leading proposition; as, "James, *who had been on the watch*, espied a sail:" if not so connected, they assert an entirely independent proposition; as, "Stephen sailed for Florida, but *he was wrecked on the voyage*." In these sentences the words in *italics* are clauses.

What is a Relative Clause?

A clause containing a relative pronoun; as, "James, *for whom I felt so much anxiety*, has arrived."

What is a Participial Clause?

A clause containing a participle; as, "*The rest of the company having arrived*, we went to dinner."

What is an Adverbial Clause?

A clause that performs the office of an adverb, and generally expresses time, place, or manner; as, "*A thousand years hence*, all these things will have passed away."

What is a Vocative Clause?

A clause containing the name of an object addressed, with its adjuncts; as, "*My dear friend*, I hope to meet you soon."

When is one noun said to be *in apposition* with another?

When it refers to the same object, and is in the same construction; as, "Paul, the Apostle"— *Apostle* is in apposition with Paul.

May a sentence contain more than one of the clauses enumerated above?

It may.

Does every sentence contain one of these clauses?

No; there are some simple sentences that do not

contain any of these clauses; as, "I love my mother."

Tell to what class each of the following sentences belongs. When a clause occurs, tell what kind of a clause it is.

1. Oh! for a lodge in some vast wilderness!

2. There are men in the world, who are dead to every generous impulse.

3. Have you heard the news that has just been received by the steamer?

4. Rising from his seat, the monarch gazed around; and, darting a look of scorn on his humbled courtiers, bade them leave his presence till they should become honest men.

5. My son, do you indulge in anger?

6. O Romeo, Romeo! wherefore art thou Romeo?

7. Who ever hears of fat men heading a riot, or herding together in turbulent mobs?

8. It is chiefly through books that we enjoy intercourse with superior minds.

9. The ship being now under sail, the shore began to recede rapidly from our sight.

10. Lord Hastings, who had borne himself most bravely throughout the whole battle, escaped with a slight wound.

11. James, whom I sent to the river an hour ago, has not yet returned.

12. What an accident! Did you ever witness a scene like this?

13. Where Freedom rears her banner, a new empire has arisen.

PUNCTUATION.

LESSON XXIII.

PERIOD, INTERROGATION-POINT, EXCLAMATION-POINT.

WHAT is Punctuation?

Punctuation is the art of dividing written language by points, in order that the meaning may be readily understood.

What are the characters used in Punctuation?

Period,	Semicolon,	
Interrogation, ?	Comma,	
Exclamation,	Dash,	
Colon,	Parentheses,	( )
	Brackets, [ ]	

Learn these characters perfectly, so that you can make them on the black-board. Turn to the oral exercise at the end of the last lesson, and mention the names of the points as they occur.

Where should the period be used?

A period should be placed after every declarative and imperative sentence; as, "*The child is asleep.*" The period is also used to denote an abbreviation; thus, when we write *Dr* for *Doctor*, or *Geo* for *George*, we must use a period—*Dr. Geo.*

Where should the interrogation-point be used?

An interrogation-point should be placed after every interrogative sentence; as, "*Have you been to Ohio?*"

Where should the exclamation-point be used?

An exclamation-point should be placed after every exclamatory sentence, and after every interjection except *O;* as, *"Alas! woe is me!"*

EXERCISE.

Write the following sentences, and insert periods, interrogation-points, and exclamation-points, in their proper places.

EXAMPLE. Alas true friendship has departed from earth

Punctuated. Alas! true friendship has departed from earth.

1. Hark the bee winds her small but mellow horn
2. What art thou doing Is revenge so sweet
3. Ha at the gates what grisly forms appear
4. Farewell ye gilded follies welcome ye silent groves
5. What would I have you do I'll tell you, kinsman; learn to be wise
6. Canst thou not sing Send forth a hymn of praise
7. No more I'll hear no more Begone
8. How dead the vegetable kingdom lies
9. The village dogs bark at the early pilgrim
10. Can you recall time that is gone Why then do you not improve the passing moments
11. A brave man knows no fear
12. Both stars and sun will fade away; but can the soul of man die
13. Oh horrible thought Ah woe is me
14. Dr Johnson was a learned man
15. New Holland contains many singular species of birds

LESSON XXIV.

COLON AND SEMICOLON.

Make a colon on the black-board.

Where should the colon be placed?

The colon should be placed between clauses that have very little connection; and after the words, *thus*, *following*, or *as follows*, when reference is made by them to something coming after; as, "The Squire next ascended the platform, and spoke as follows: 'Gentlemen and ladies,'" &c.

Make a semicolon on the black-board.

For what is the semicolon used?

The semicolon is used to separate long clauses, and such as are not very closely connected; as, "I perceive the difference; it is very obvious."

Special Rules.

Rule I. When several long clauses follow each other, all having common dependence on some other clause, they are separated by semicolons; as, "I love to wander through the fields; to see the vegetable world spring into life; to gaze upon the beauties which God has so lavishly diffused; and through the creature to commune with the Creator."

Rule II. When examples are introduced by the word *as*, a semicolon is placed before *as;* for an example, see the preceding rule.

EXERCISE.

Write the following sentences, and insert

periods, interrogation-points, exclamation-points, colons, and semicolons, where they are required:—

EXAMPLE. He has arrived he sounds his bugle at the gates   Shall we admit him

Punctuated. He has arrived; he sounds his bugle at the gates.   Shall we admit him?

1. The warrior spoke as follows " O man heavy with wine why dost thou thus keep prattling "

2. Do not insult a poor man his misery entitles him to pity

3. Some books are to be read others are to be studied while many may be entirely neglected with positive advantage

4. His last words were as follows " Farewell may Heaven prosper thee in thy perilous enterprise "

5. If the sacred writers will take up their abode under my roof if Milton will cross my threshold, to sing to me of Paradise if Shakspeare will open to me the fields of imagination I shall not pine for want of company

6. Beauty is an all-pervading presence   It unfolds in the flowers of spring it waves in the branches of the trees it haunts the depths of the earth and sea

7. Gentle reader, have you ever sailed on the sparkling waters of the Mississippi

LESSON XXV.

COMMA.

MAKE a comma on the black-board.
For what is the comma used ?

The comma is used to separate short clauses, or such as are closely connected, but, in consequence of the construction or arrangement, must be separated by some point.

SPECIAL RULES. What is the rule for placing the comma before and after clauses and phrases ?

Rule I. When a clause or phrase is introduced into a sentence without a conjunction, particularly if an inversion occurs, so that it does not occupy its natural position, a comma should be placed before and after it ; or, if such clause stands at the commencement of a sentence, a comma should be placed after it.

The principal clauses and phrases that fall under this rule are as follows :—

I. A relative clause ; as, "Ellen, who was up early, finished her lessons." But if the relative clause restricts the antecedent, or the connection between the two is very close, there is no comma before the relative ; as, "Those who are good, are happy."

II. A participial clause when it does not qualify the object of a verb ; as, "The Captain, seeing his danger, avoided it."

III. An adverbial clause ; as, "By the time we reached shelter, we were completely wet."

IV. A vocative clause ; as, "Here I am, my beloved son."

V. The phrases, *in short, in truth, on the contrary,* &c. ; also, the words, *besides, moreover, namely, nay, firstly, secondly,* &c. The conjunctions *also* and *however,* which should not commence a sentence, have a comma before and after them ; as, "Your cousin, in short, has become a lovely woman." "James, however, is here."

What is the rule that relates to the subject of a verb ?

Rule II. When the subject of a verb consists

of a number of words, a comma should be placed after it; as, " Close and undivided attention to any object, insures success."

What is the rule that relates to the omission of words?

Rule III. When, to avoid repetition, a verb, or a conjunction that connects words of the same part of speech, is omitted, a comma should be put in its place to denote the omission; as, " Conversation makes a ready man; writing, an exact man." In the last clause the verb *makes* is omitted, and a comma is put in its place. " Solomon was a wise, prudent, and powerful monarch." The conjunction *and* is omitted between *wise* and *prudent*, and a comma is put in its place.

What is the rule that relates to certain conjunctions?

Rule IV. A comma should be placed before *and*, *or*, *if*, *but*, and *that*, when they connect short clauses; and before *and*, *or*, and *nor*, when they connect the last two of a series of words that are of the same part of speech; as, " You must come with me, or I will go with you." " Neither Ellen, Sarah, nor Jane, was there."

What is the rule that relates to nouns in apposition?

Rule V. When a clause of more than two words occurs, containing a noun in apposition with some preceding noun, a comma should be placed before and after the clause; as, " Columbus, the discoverer of America, was born in Genoa."

What is the rule that relates to words used in pairs?

Rule VI. Words used in pairs take a comma after each pair; as, " Poverty and distress, desolation and ruin, are the consequences of civil war."

Copy the following sentences, and insert commas in the proper places. The rule under which the examples are given, will direct you; refer to it, if you do not remember it.

Examples under Rule I. The Romans, who conquered the world could not conquer themselves. Those who fled, were killed. Philip, whose wife you have seen, has gone to Albany. We saw a man, walking on the rails. A man while imprudently walking on the rails was run over by the cars. Where we stood, we could not hear a word. Wait a moment, my friend. Vice is alluring, and has many votaries; virtue on the contrary has but few.

Under Rule II. That this man has basely deceived those who have trusted him can not be doubted. A long life of good works and sincere repentance can hardly atone for such misdeeds. The author of these profound and learned philosophical essays was a poor blacksmith.

Under Rule III. Diligence is the mother of success; laziness of failure. The wife was a tall lean cadaverous personage; the husband was a fine good-looking sturdy fellow. Men women and children stare cry out and run.

Under Rule IV. No one will respect you if you are dishonest. Stephen saw his cousin coming and ran to meet her. My horse is not handsome but he trots well. He will be here on Wednesday Thursday or Friday. Be virtuous that you may be esteemed by your companions.

Under Rule V. Bunyan the author of "The Pilgrim's Progress" was a tinker. Paul the Apostle of the Gentiles wrote many epistles. I have been in Ireland ill-fated country. Cicero the orator is one of the most distinguished of the ancient Romans.

Under Rule VI. Industry and virtue idleness and vice go hand in hand. Summer and winter seed-time and harvest are the gifts of an all-wise Providence. Painting and sculpture poetry and music will always have enthusiastic admirers.

LESSON XXVI.

EXERCISE.

Copy and punctuate the following extract :—

THE SWAN.

Swans in a wild state are found in the eastern part of Europe but they are most abundant in Siberia and the countries that surround the Caspian Sea Under ordinary circumstances they are perfectly harmless but when driven to act on the defensive have proved themselves formidable enemies. They have great strength in their wings an old swan using these as his weapons has been known to break a man's leg with a single stroke When their young are in danger they do not hesitate to engage with large animals and not unfrequently come off victorious from the struggle A female swan was once seen to attack and drown a fox which was swimming toward her nest for the purpose of feeding upon her young

When sailing on the water which is its favorite element the swan is a beautiful bird and its motions are graceful when seen on land however it presents a very different appearance its gait being awkward and all its movements exceedingly clumsy

It has been said by some authors that the swan which

during its life never sings a note sends forth when it is dying a most beautiful strain   This is no doubt a mere fable at all events we have not sufficient evidence to establish it as a fact

Swans were formerly held in such esteem in England that by an act of Edward IV no one but the king's son was permitted to keep a swan unless he had an income of five marks a year   By a subsequent act those who took their eggs were punished by imprisonment for a year and a day and fined according to the king's pleasure   At the present day swans are little valued for the delicacy of their flesh though many are still preserved for their beauty

LESSON XXVII.

DASH, PARENTHESES, BRACKETS.

Make a dash.

For what is the dash used?

The dash is used,

I. To denote that a sentence is unfinished; as, " I can not believe that he ———."

II. To denote a sudden transition either in the form of a sentence or in the sentiment expressed; as, " It was a sight—that child in the agony of death—that would have moved a heart of stone."

> " He had no malice in his mind—
> No ruffles on his shirt."

Make parentheses.   Make brackets.

For what are parentheses and brackets used?

Parentheses and brackets are used to enclose words and clauses, that are not connected in construction with other words in the sentence, but are suggested by them, or explanatory of their meaning ; as,

"Know, then, this truth (enough for man to know),
 Virtue alone is happiness below."

"The wisest men (and it may be said the best too) are not exempt from sin."

Are parentheses and brackets much used by authors at the present day ?

No ; commas are generally used instead of them.

EXERCISE.

Copy and punctuate the following sentences :—
Dash.

1. A crimson handkerchief adorned his head
   His face was cheerful and his nose was red

2. Some and they were not a few melt down

3. His eyes how they twinkled his dimples how merry

4. They poisoned my very soul hot burning poisons

5. Away ungrateful wretch   A father's curse rest Alas what am I doing   I can not curse my son

6. The friend of our infancy has she gone forever

7.   Thou merry laughing sprite
           With spirits feather light
   Untouched by sorrow and unsoiled by sin
   Good Heavens the child is swallowing a pin
           Thou imp of mirth and joy
   In love's dear chain so strong and bright a link
   Thou idol of thy parents   drat the boy
           There goes my ink

Parentheses.

8. Let us then for we cannot flee without disgrace boldly meet the foe

9. Mr. Morton every old citizen knows him well died last week of apoplexy

LESSON XXVIII.

OTHER MARKS USED IN WRITING.

ARE any other marks used in writing, besides those which have been described?

Yes;

Apostrophe,	Hyphen, -
Quotation-points, " "	Caret, ∧

Make an apostrophe. For what is the apostrophe used?

The apostrophe is used,

I. To denote the omission of one or more letters; as, *tho'* for *though; 'neath* for *beneath.*

II. When *s* is placed after a noun, making it denote possession, an apostrophe is inserted before the *s;* as *John's book.* But when the noun ends in *s*, and signifies more than one, an apostrophe alone placed after it makes it denote possession; as, " The ladies' seats ".

Make quotation-points. For what are quotation-points used?

Quotation-points are used to enclose a passage quoted from an author or speaker, in his own words; as,

" To err is human; to forgive, divine."

Are single quotation-points (' ') ever used?

Yes; single quotation-points are used to enclose

quotations that occur within quotations, or that are slightly altered from the words of the author or speaker; as, " The Scripture saith, ' Watch and pray.' "

Make a hyphen. For what is the hyphen used?

The hyphen is used,

I. To connect two simple words that unite to form a compound word; as, " A spirit-moving strain".

II. At the end of a line, when there is not room for the whole of a word, the hyphen is placed after one of its syllables, to show that the remainder may be found at the beginning of the next line;*   as, " He strove manfully."

Make a caret. For what is the caret used?

When some word that has been omitted is interlined, the caret is used to show where it should be introduced; as, " Study this ^{lesson} carefully."
                                          ^

EXERCISE.

Copy and punctuate the following sentences :—

Apostrophe. I'll neer forget your kindness. They sat neath a spreading willow. Tho Milton was blind yet was his mind well stored with knowledge. Hark tis the signal gun. Where is my fathers hat? Zenos school was one of the most celebrated in Greece. Romes great-

---

* When the pupil, in writing, can not get the whole of a word in the line, and has to carry part of it to the next, he must be careful to divide it according to its syllables, and place the hyphen after a complete syllable.

ness has passed away.   I saw the citys gates.   I saw the cities gates.   Where is Janes fan?

Quotation-points.   Pope says The proper study of mankind is man. When Socrates was asked what man approached the nearest to perfect happiness he answered That man who has the fewest wants.   The philosopher hath truly said Anxiety is the poison of human life.   The quality of mercy says Shakspeare is not strained.   How much truth there is in Franklin's maxim One to-day is worth two to-morrows.

Hyphen.   Away thou earth polluting miscreant! He is a mischief maker.   The laborer enjoys his well earned feast.   The air is full of snow flakes.   Where is your eye glass?   Near the shore was a grove of spice wood.   The river glides on in its serpent like course.

Caret.   (*In each of the following sentences, one or more words are omitted.   Introduce the omitted word*
                                            is
or words by means of a caret; as, Dark the path.)

Labor gives a relish pleasure.   Hope, the balm life, soothes under every misfortune.   Charity is one of the of virtues.   Always show to the aged.   Honor your father mother.   Do not your time.

LESSON XXIX.

EXERCISE.

Copy and punctuate the following extracts:—

1. PHOCION.—Phocion one of the most illustrious of the ancient Greeks was condemned to death by his un-

grateful countrymen   When about to drink the fatal hemlock he was asked if he had any thing to say to his son   Bring him before me cried he   My dear son said this magnanimous patriot I entreat you to serve your country as faithfully as I have done and to forget that she rewarded my services with an unjust death.

2. THE SYBARITES.—We have heard many stories of lazy people but what Athenæus tells us of the Sybarites a nation of antiquity exceeds them all. They would not allow any mechanical trade to be carried on in their city because the noise was unpleasant and disturbed their slumbers for the same reason to keep a rooster was a grave offence punishable by law. A Sybarite on one occasion it is said wandering out into the country saw some men digging whereupon the sight gave him a violent strain in the back while a friend to whom he described what he had seen caught a severe pain in the side.   One of them having visited Lacedæmon was introduced to the public table where the principal dish was *black broth*. Ah cried he no longer do I wonder at the bravery of the Spartans for rather would I die than live on such wretched diet.

3. THE FORM OF THE EARTH.—Heraclitus supposed that the earth had the form of a canoe Aristotle that it was shaped like a timbrel while Anaximander proved to his own satisfaction that it was a vast cylinder.   It was reserved for a later age to discover its real shape

LESSON XXX.

EXERCISE.

Copy and punctuate the following extract :—

THE LEPROSY IN AFRICA. Leprosy that awful disease which covers the body with scales still exists in Africa Whether it is the same leprosy as that mentioned in the Bible is not known but it is regarded as perfectly incurable and so infectious that no one dares to come near the leper In the south of Africa there is a large lazar ho e for the victims of this terrible malady It consists an immense space enclosed by a very high wall an ntaining fields which the lepers cultivate There is only one entrance and it is strictly guarded When any one is found with the marks of leprosy upon him he is brought to this gate and enters never to return Within this abode of misery there are multitudes of lepers in all stages of the disease Dr Helbeck a missionary of the Church of England from the top of a neighboring hill saw them at work He noticed two particularly sowing peas in the field The one had no hands the other no feet those members having been wasted away by the disease The one who wanted the hands was carrying the other who wanted the feet on his back and he again bore in his hands the bag of seed and dropped a pea every now and then which the other pressed into the ground with his foot and so they managed the work of one man between the two

Such is the prison house of disease Ah how little do we realize the misery that is in the world How unthankful are we for the blessings which God bestows upon us while He denies them to others

LESSON XXXI.

RULES FOR THE USE OF CAPITAL LETTERS.

WHAT usage formerly prevailed with regard to capital letters?

To begin every noun, both in writing and printing, with a capital. This is still the practice in the German language.

What are the rules that are to guide us at the present day?

Begin with a capital letter,

1. The first word of every sentence.

2. All proper nouns, and titles of office or honor; as, *Rome, Spain, President Fillmore, General Washington, Henry Street.*

3. Adjectives formed from proper nouns; as, *Roman, Spanish.*

4. Common nouns when spoken to, or spoken of, as persons; as, " *Come, gentle Spring.*"

5. The first word of every line of poetry.

6. The appellations of the Deity, and personal pronouns standing for His name; as, " *God is the Lord ; He ruleth in His might.*"

7. The first word of a quotation that forms a complete sentence by itself, and is not introduced by *that*, or other words which would connect it in construction with what precedes; as, " *Remember the old maxim : ' Honesty is the best policy.'* "

8. Every important word in the titles of books, or headings of chapters; as " *Locke's Essay on the Human Understanding.*"

9. Words that are the leading subjects of discourse.

10. The pronoun *I*, and the interjection *O*, must be written in capitals.

Copy the following sentences, applying the rules given above, and observing that where there is no rule for using a capital you must substitute a small letter:—

1. *Under Rule I.* know Thyself. honesty is the best policy. follow virtue. It Rains. envy is a Dishonorable emotion. avoid the appearance of evil. improve every Moment.

2. *Under Rules II. and III.* Alexander the great overran syria, persia, lydia, and hyrcania, pushing his Conquests as far as the river indus. napoleon kept all europe at bay, until the Fatal Field of waterloo consigned him to st. helena. President adams received the congratulations of the french and spanish ministers.

3. *Under Rule IV.* Hail, winter, seated on thine icy Throne! Fierce war has sounded his trumpet, And Called the peasant from the field. bland Goddess peace now smiles upon the plain. here I and sorrow sit. Grim darkness furls his leaden Shroud.

4. *Under Rules V. and VI.*

   in every leaf that trembles to the breeze,
   i hear the Voice of god among the trees.
   Trust in the lord; hath he Spoken, and shall he not do it?
   these, as they change, almighty father, these
   are but the varied god.

5. *Under Rule VII.* This was our saviour's command: "watch and pray." Virgil says, "labor conquers all things." "merry christmas," cried the delighted villagers.

6. *Under Rule VIII.* milton's "paradise lost" brought him in only twenty-eight Pounds. Have you read dickens' Account of his visit to america, which he entitles "american notes for general circulation"? I have read with delight hervey's "meditations among the tombs".

7. *Under Rule X.* i love thee not as once ˙ loved, false friend, o cruel traitor. O Heaven! am undone! O wretched youth! I thought i hated thee; but thy misfortune hath turned My Hate To Pity.

LESSON XXXII.

A REVIEW.

WHAT is a sentence? How many kinds of sentences are there? What is a declarative sentence? an imperative sentence? an interrogative sentence? an exclamatory sentence?

What is a phrase? What is a clause? What is a relative clause? a participial clause? an adverbial clause? a vocative clause?

When is one noun said to be in apposition with another?

What is punctuation? Name the characters used in punctuation. Where is the period placed? What is the period also used to denote? Where is the interrogation-point used? the exclamation-point? Where should the colon be placed? What is the semicolon used to separate? Repeat the rule for the use of the semicolon between dependent clauses; the rule that relates to examples.

For what is the comma used? What is the rule that relates to the use of the comma in the case of clauses and phrases? What are the four principal clauses that fall under this rule? Mention some of the phrases that fall under it. What is the rule that relates to the subject of a verb? to the omission of words? to certain conjunctions? to nouns in apposition? to words used in pairs?

EXERCISE.

Copy the following extracts, inserting, as may be required, capital letters, punctuation-points, and the other marks used in writing, described in Lesson XXVIII.:—

1. The Bushman and the missionary.—the bushmen are a very degraded and ignorant race who live in southern africa not far from the cape of good hope, A missionary who for some time had been laboring to introduce christianity among them took occasion one day to speak of the great objects of creation and the duties of man at last he asked, what is the chief end of man The bushmen were silent for several moments apparently reflecting what answer they should give to this difficult question At length one of them who seemed inspired by a sudden idea replied, to steal oxen

2. The bravery of Horatius cocles.—when porsenna king of the etrurians was endeavoring to reëstablish tarquinius superbus on the throne he attacked rome and had the good fortune to take the janiculum at the first assault At this crisis horatius cocles a common sentinel but a man of the greatest courage posted himself at the extremity of the Sublician bridge and alone withstood the whole force of the enemy till the bridge was broken down behind him he then threw himself into the tiber and swam over to his friends unhurt by either his fall or the darts of the enemy

3.   by wisdom tutored poetry exalts,
       her voice to ages and informs the page,
       with music image sentiment and thought
       never to die.

LESSON XXXIII.

A REVIEW.

For what is the dash used? For what are parentheses and brackets used? For what is the apostrophe used? quotation-points? the hyphen? the caret?

Repeat the ten rules for the use of capital letters.

EXERCISE.

Copy the following extracts, inserting, as may be required, capitals, punctuation-points, and the other marks used in writing :—

Liars.—aristides among the athenians and epaminondas among the thebans are said to have been such lovers of truth that they never told a lie even in joke. atticus likewise with whom cicero was very intimate neither told a lie himself nor could bear it in others. i hate that man achilles used to say as much as I do the gates of pluto who says one thing and thinks another. Aristotle bears his testimony as follows liars are not believed even when they speak the truth. Sincerity is one of the most important virtues that man can possess.

The Affectionate Dolphin.—during the reign of the emperor augustus a dolphin formed an attachment to the son of a poor man who used to feed him with bits of bread. every day the dolphin when called by the boy swam to the surface of the water and after having received his usual meal carried the boy on his ack from baiæ to a school in puteoli and brought him back in the same manner. The boy after a time died and the dolphin coming to the usual place and missing is kind master is said also to have died of grief.

LESSON XXXIV.

PRIMITIVE, COMPOUND, AND DERIVATIVE WORDS.
ANALYSIS.—ACCENT.

WHAT is a Word?

A Word is what is written or spoken as the sign of an idea.

Into how many classes may we divide words, when considered with regard to their origin?

Into three classes; Primitive, Compound, and Derivative.

What is a Primitive Word?

A **Primitive Word** is one that is not formed from any simpler word; as, *watch, man.*

What is a Compound Word?

A **Compound Word** is one that is formed by uniting two or more words; as, *watchman.*

What is a Derivative Word?

A **Derivative Word** is one that is formed from a single primitive; as, *watches, manly.*

How are derivatives formed from primitives?

By the addition of one or more letters; which, if placed before the primitive, are called *prefixes ;* if after it, suffixes. Thus, *act* is a primitive; *transact* is a derivative, formed by the addition of the prefix *trans ; acted* is a derivative, formed by the addition of the suffix *ed.*

What is meant by analyzing a word?

Separating it into parts.

Analyze the word *walking.*

Walking is a derivative, formed of the primitive *walk* and the suffix *ing.*

Analyze the word *man-hater*.

Man-hater is a compound word, formed of the two words *man* and *hater*.

Analyze *blindly, review, glass-house, moreover, bird-cage, repress*.

What mark is generally used to connect the primitives that unite to form a compound word?

The hyphen.

What is meant by Accent?

By **Accent** is meant stress of voice: thus, in *colder*, the first syllable, *cold*, receives the stress of the voice, and therefore we say that the accent is on *cold*.

On how many syllables in a word may accent be laid?

In short words, on one syllable only; as, *ra*ven, be*gin*, de*ny*. In long words, besides the principal accent, a secondary accent may be laid on some other syllable or syllables; as, *agricul*ture, *Con*stantinople, incompre*hensibi*lity.

In *scholar*, which syllable is accented? in *dethrone?* in *misery?* in *civilize?* in *inhabitant?* in *philosophy?*

EXERCISE.

Primitive Words. Night, day, school, book, store, fruit, fire, man, boat, sun, flower, garden, ice, glass, green, house.

1. Form and write out ten compound words, by uniting two of the above primitives. You are not at liberty to unite *any* two, but only such as form a compound word that makes good sense, or that you may have seen or heard used. Thus, *night-book* would not do; but *night-school* would convey a definite idea, and would be proper.

2. Form and write out ten derivative words from the

primitives given above, by adding to them the suffix *s*, *ly*, or *ing;* as, *nights, daily, schooling.*

3. Write out six words accented on the first sylla- ble; as, *writing, sunny.*

4. Write out six words accented on the second syl- lable; as, *affirm, destroy.*

5. Write out six words accented on the third sylla- ble; as, *elevation, Alabama.*

LESSON XXXV.

SPELLING.—RULES.

WHAT is Spelling?

Spelling is the art of expressing words by their proper letters.

Are words spelled as we would expect to find them, from their pronunciation?

Sometimes they are, but not always.

What is the best method of becoming a good speller?

A person may become a good speller,

I. By carefully observing the words with which he meets, while reading.

II. When he is writing, by looking out in a dictionary all the words respecting which he has any doubt.

Does the dictionary contain every word that you may have occasion to use?

Not every word; there are some derivatives which it does not contain.

How, then, are you to know how to spell these derivatives?

There are certain rules which direct us as to their formation.

What is the need of these rules? If we can spell the primitive and the prefix or suffix, may we not simply join them together and spell the derivative?

In some cases we may; but, often, a change is made in a primitive before a suffix is added. Thus, in forming *having* from *have*, the *e* of the primitive *have* is rejected, before the suffix *ing* is added. The rules cover such cases as this.

When no rule applies, how do you form a derivative?

Regularly; that is, without making any change before adding the prefix or suffix.

How many important rules are there?

Four.

When is a letter said to be *final?*

When it has the last letter in a word; thus, in *have* there is a final *e.*

Mention four words that have final vowels; four that have final consonants.

Repeat the rule that relates to final *e.*

Rule I. The final *e* of a primitive word is rejected before a suffix beginning with a vowel; as, *hate, hating*—the final *e* of *hate* is rejected before the suffix *ing*, which begins with a vowel.

Form and spell the derivatives that are obtained by adding the suffix *ing* to the primitives, *rave, shave, hope, smoke.*

Repeat the rule that relates to the final consonant of a monosyllable.

Rule II. The final consonant of a monosyllable, if preceded by a single vowel, is doubled before a suffix beginning with a vowel; as, *hat, hatter.* In this example, the final *t* of the monosyllable *hat* is preceded by a single vowel, a, and is doubled before the suffix *er.*

Form and spell the derivatives that are obtained by adding the suffix *er* to the primitives, *chat, hot, spin, win.*

Repeat the rule that relates to the final consonant of any word accented on the last syllable.

Rule III. The final consonant of any word accented on the last syllable, if preceded by a single vowel, is doubled before a suffix beginning with a vowel; as, *debar, debarring. Debar* is accented on the last syllable; the final consonant, *r,* is preceded by a single vowel, and is doubled before the suffix *ing.*

Form and spell the derivatives that are obtained by adding the suffix *ed* to the primitives, *abhor, rebut, remit, permit.*

Repeat the rule that relates to final *y.*

Rule IV. The final *y* of a primitive word, when preceded by a consonant, is changed into *i,* before a suffix which does not commence with *i ;* as, *glory, glorious.* The final *y* of *glory* is preceded by the consonant *r,* and is changed into *i* before the suffix *ous,* which does not commence with *i.* When the suffix commences with *i,* the final *y* remains unchanged; as, *glory, glorying.*

When *y* final is preceded by a *vowel,* is it changed into *i* upon the addition of a suffix?

No, it remains unchanged; as, *joy, joyous ; play, playing.*

EXERCISE.

Under Rule I. Write out the derivatives that are obtained by adding the suffix *ing* to the following words : rule, trace, strike, bite, invite, plunge, censure, tolerate, unite, blame, rebuke, allure.

Under Rule II. Write out the derivatives that are

obtained by adding the suffix *ed* to the following words:
pin, shun, plot, plan, spot, tan, dip, fit, sin, thin, hop, jar.

Under Rule III. Write out the derivatives that are
obtained by adding the suffix *ing* to the following
words: begin, unpin, abet, debar, occur, admit, confer,
recur, compel, unfit, dispel, deter.

Under Rule IV. Write out the derivatives that
are obtained by adding the suffix *ed* to the following
words: cry, try, fry, deny, multiply, terrify, dry, busy,
copy, defy, empty, remedy.

Miscellaneous Exercise. Write out the derivatives
that are obtained by adding the suffix *ing* to the following words: brave, destroy,* play, charge, judge,
employ, annoy, stay, permit, unbar, refer, number,†
profit, alter, propel, flatter, mar, stir, transmit, drive,
justify,‡ decry, say.

LESSON XXXVI.

SUBJECT AND PREDICATE.

You have now learned how to punctuate, and
when it is proper to use capital letters; you have
also had rules for the formation of such derivatives
as are not in the dictionary. You are, therefore,
prepared to make sentences of your own.

---

* Observe that here *a vowel* comes before final *y;* other words
like this will be given.

† Observe that this word is accented on the *first* syllable; the
final consonant, therefore, is not doubled. Other words like this
will be given.

‡ Remember that the final *y* remains unchanged before a suffix
commencing with *i.*

What is a Sentence ?

A Sentence is such an assemblage of words as makes complete sense.

Of how many parts does every sentence consist ?

Of two parts, Subject and Predicate.

What is the Subject of a sentence ?

The **Subject** of a sentence is that respecting which something is affirmed.

What is the Predicate ?

The **Predicate** is that which is affirmed respecting the subject.

Select the subject and predicate in the sentence, "*Intemperance leads to destruction.*"

Intemperance is the subject, because something is affirmed respecting it ; *leads to destruction* is the predicate, because it affirms something about the subject, *intemperance.*

What part of speech affirms ?

A verb.

What must there be, then, in every sentence ?

A verb.

Before beginning to write sentences of your own, it will be well for you to learn the following directions, which, if carefully attended to, will be found of great service :—

I. Be sure to use punctuation-points and capitals, according to the rules which have been given.

II. Take care that every word is spelled correctly ; use your dictionary whenever you are in doubt, and apply the four rules that relate to the formation of derivative words.

III. If you date your composition, put a comma after the name of the place, a comma after the day of the month, and a period after the year ; thus, *New York, November* 1*st,* 1868.

IV. Never write in a hurry or carelessly ; but do your best to make each composition better than the preceding one.

V. After you have written your composition, look over it with care, in order to correct whatever errors you may have committed, in punctuation, in spelling, or in style.

EXERCISE.

Write sentences containing the following words. When you can, introduce two or more of the words into the same sentence.

EXAMPLE. Write sentences containing the words, *day, hour, moment, friendship, neglect.*

Sentences. Each *day,* each *hour,* each *moment,* should be diligently improved.

Cultivate the *friendship* of the good.

Neglect not your studies.

Handsome,	crowd,	poor,	country,
graceful,	market,	wretched,	fields,
industry,	flowers,	gentle,	covered,
success,	fruit,	kind,	virtuous,
diligent,	pleasure,	companions,	esteem,
obtain,	reading,	quickly,	respect,
reward,	try,	expect,	ridiculed,
winter,	excel,	discovered,	school,
dreary,	kind,	frightened,	houses,
appears,	heart,	fainted,	city,
influence,	terrible,	education,	noise.

LESSON XXXVII.

EXERCISE.

WRITE sentences containing the following combinations of words :—

EXAMPLE. Write sentences containing the words, *severe affliction, walking alone.*

Sentences. The loss of his fortune was a *severe affliction.*

While *walking alone* in the woods, I met a panther.

Hard study. A strong dislike. No confidence can be placed. Where the house now stands. On the ocean. A dangerous undertaking. Ignorance and vice. I would rather. Those who do their duty. Begging in the street. Geography furnishes us. Astronomy teaches us. Birds' nests. A storm at sea. To preserve our health. It is hard work. The life of the merchant. Fought bravely. Produces happiness. A large clock. The tops of high mountains. A band of robbers. If it rain. When my father returns. Are very useful. We seldom see. Always show respect. Large farms produce. Exercises in composition. Very important.

LESSON XXXVIII.

SENTENCES CONTAINING RELATIVE AND PARTICIPIAL CLAUSES.

WHAT is a relative clause?

What is a participial clause?

Who, which, and *that,* are relative pronouns; what is to be observed in using them?

Who is used, when the antecedent is the name of a person; *which*, when it is the name of an inferior animal, or an object without life; *that* is used in either case. Thus, the *boy who* studies;

the *house which* stands ; the *man that* is virtuous ; the *dog that* barks.

What is the rule for using commas in the case of relative and participial clauses ?   (See Rule I., page 59.)

EXERCISE.

Write sentences containing the following relative and participial clauses :—

EXAMPLE.   Who made many scientific discoveries. In examining witnesses.

Sentences.   Sir Isaac Newton, *who made many scientific discoveries,* was buried in Westminster Abbey.

Much time was spent *in examining witnesses.*

RELATIVE CLAUSES Those * who are virtuous.   The man who attends diligently to business. Which I found in the street. Whom I esteem very highly. That barks at the slightest noise. Which was wrecked at sea. Whose father I much respected. Who recites his lessons well. All that I have Whose character is excellent. The person who reads good books. The city in which we live. The country in which we live. Who defeated the enemy. Which was given me by a friend.

PARTICIPIAL CLAUSES. The weather being pleasant. The rain having ceased. The river having overflowed its banks. The boat having started. The enemy having fled. My brother having returned. The carriage having been broken. While walking by the river. While travelling through Ohio. Run over by a stage. Hundreds of men lying on the battle-field. Playing and shouting in the street. Overcome by fatigue. Accom-

* The pupil will observe that in this case, and some others, the antecedent is given.

panied by a friend. In studying mathematics. By attending to your studies. By reading good books. In doing good. In buying and selling goods. Having arrived at Boston.

LESSON XXXIX.

SENTENCES CONTAINING ADVERBIAL AND VOCA-TIVE CLAUSES.

WHAT is an adverbial clause? Give an example.

What is a vocative clause? Give an example.

What is the rule for using commas in the case of adverbial and vocative clauses? (See Rule I., page 59.)

EXERCISE.

Write sentences containing the following adverbial and vocative clauses :—

EXAMPLE. Before I arrived. Gentlemen and ladies.

Sentences. The vessel had started *before I arrived. Gentlemen and ladies*, I ask your attention to a very important subject.

ADVERBIAL CLAUSES. A hundred years hence. Where we live. In a very improper manner. With great unwillingness. Before the vessel arrived in port. When the election was held. In the school which I attend Before Columbus discovered America. When we finish our lessons. When the lecturer commenced. When the boat lands. During the summer months. After winter has set in. With great care. After the storm occurred. When a man has a bad character. In a book which I have read. Where the river rises. In a disagreeable manner. Without any delay. Immediately after the battle. When a country has a tyrannical government.

VOCATIVE CLAUSES. My friend. My dear Sir. You disagreeable fellow. My dear Mary.

––––⚬––––

LESSON XL.

DIFFERENT KINDS OF SENTENCES.

How many kinds of sentences are there? (See page 52.)
What are they?
What is a declarative sentence? an imperative sentence? an interrogative sentence? an exclamatory sentence?
May a declarative sentence be turned into an imperative, an interrogative, or an exclamatory sentence?

It may.

Give me an example.

It snows, is a declarative sentence; *let it snow*, is imperative; *does it snow?* is interrogative; and *how it snows!* is exclamatory.

What word is generally used to introduce an imperative sentence?

Let. Thus: " *Let* there be silence ; " " *Let* us go."

What words are used to introduce an interrogative sentence?

The interrogative pronouns, and the words, *is, was, does, did, has, will.* Thus: " *Is* my son here?" " *Does* he study his lessons?" " *Will* you be there?"

What words are used to introduce exclamatory sentences?

How and *what.* Thus: " *How* disagreeable he is!" " *What* a disagreeable man he is!"

EXERCISE.

Convert the following *declarative* into the corresponding *interrogative* and *exclamatory* sentences :

EXAMPLE. Milton was a great poet.

Interrogative. Was Milton a great poet?

Exclamatory. What a great poet Milton was!

1. Sir Isaac Newton was a great philosopher.
2. Benjamin Franklin wrote many excellent maxims.
3. A good boy will study hard to learn his lesson.
4. Pope has left us many admirable lines.
5. America has attained a desirable rank among the nations of the world.
6. Julia entered the parlor gracefully.
7. Philadelphia is a large city.
8. Gratitude is a noble emotion.

Convert the following *declarative* into the corresponding *interrogative* and *imperative* sentences :—

EXAMPLE. Stephen prepares his lesson well.

Interrogative. Does Stephen prepare his lesson well?

Imperative. Let Stephen prepare his lesson well.

9. The army marches.
10. The dog barks.
11. The cannon roar in honor of victory.
12. The books are ready.
13. His good fortune makes him happy.
14. They did their duty.
15. Bees gather honey from flowers.

LESSON XLI.

EXERCISE.

WRITE six declarative, six imperative, six interrogative, and six exclamatory sentences, each of which shall contain one of the following words in order :—

EXAMPLE.   *Words—happy, speak, come, loss.*
Sentences.   Declarative—The good are *happy.*
Imperative—Let no one *speak.*
Interrogative—Has my brother *come?*
Exclamatory—What a *loss!*

Camels,	go,	arrived,	accident,
studious,	lessons,	sick,	unpleasant,
begins,	time,	books,	storm,
walking,	school,	many,	found,
graceful,	injure,	sold,	seen,
idle,	keep,	studied,	handsome.

LESSON XLII.

FORMATION OF SENTENCES.

(For the answers to these questions, see the first eleven Lessons.)

WHAT is an article? a noun? a pronoun? an adjective? a verb? an adverb? a conjunction? a preposition? an interjection?

What word prefixed to a verb shows that it is in the infinitive mood?

To ; to eat, to keep, are in the infinitive mood.

EXERCISE.

1. Write five sentences containing a subject, a transitive verb, and an object ;. as, "The *bee makes honey.*"

2. Write five sentences containing an adjective, a noun, a transitive verb, and an object; as, "The *provident ant lays* up her *store.*"

3. Write five sentences containing a subject, a transitive verb, an object, and an adverb; as, "*Louise studied* her *grammar faithfully.*"

4. Write five sentences containing a verb in the infinitive mood; as, "I tried *to learn* my lesson."

5. Write five sentences each of which shall have for its subject two nouns connected by the conjunction *and;* as, "The *lion and* the *tiger* are the fiercest of animals."

LESSON XLIII.

VARIETY OF ARRANGEMENT.

How may we obtain *variety* in a succession of sentences?

By employing a different arrangement of the words or clauses, or a different construction.

When the variety consists in the arrangement, what is it called?

Variety of Arrangement.

When the variety consists in a difference of construction, what is it called?

Variety of Expression.

EXERCISE.

Arrange the words in the following sentences differently, but in such a way that the meaning may remain the same :—

EXAMPLE.   The night was dark.
                     Paris is the capital of France.
Transposed. Dark was the night.
                     The capital of France is Paris.

1. Furious was the storm.

2. Mournfully the wind waved among the branches.

3. The longest river in Europe is the Volga.

4. Than virtue nothing is lovelier.

5. Here lies the lamented Warren.

6. Grammar teaches us to speak correctly and to write accurately.

7. Of ancient traders, the first and most expert were the Phœnicians.

8. Formerly, it required a week for a person to go from New York to Albany.

9. From Corsica the Carthaginians obtained honey and raisins.

10. At last summer has set in.

11. Suddenly a shout arose.

12. We can not prize a good character too highly.

13. Perhaps you left it at home.

14. The sheriff seized his prisoner roughly.

15. Do you not know me, Mary?

16. How careful ought we to be to avoid vice!

17. Let me go, I beseech you.

18. Generally, the North American Indians are dressed in buffalo-skins.

19. There hangs the picture of my father.

20. Here stands your servant.

LESSON XLIV.

VARIETY OF ARRANGEMENT.

EXERCISE.

ARRANGE the clauses in the following sentences differently, but in such a way that the meaning may remain the same. The pupil must remember to make such changes in the punctuation as may be required by the transposition.

EXAMPLE. Well pleased with my visit, I returned home.

Transposed. I returned home, well pleased with my visit.

1. Never put off till to-morrow what you can do to-day.

2. Sir Isaac Newton, one of the greatest mathematicians the world has ever produced, was born in Woolsthorpe, England, on Christmas day, A. D. 1642.

3. Cæsar, after having reached the pinnacle of human greatness, perished by assassination.

4. My good friend, where are you going ?

5. Washington is buried at Mount Vernon, on the banks of the Potomac River.

6. During the night, the enemy moved their camp.

7. She sunk down in the road, exhausted by fatigue.

8. Cannon were first used about 500 years ago, at the battle of Cressy.

9. By the code of Lycurgus, all the Spartans were compelled to eat at a common table.

10. In every part of Europe, we find the French language spoken.

11. While the clouds thus hid the moon from view, I heard a loud groan.

12. Improve every moment while you are in school.

13. We must strive hard, if we wish to excel.

14. If Columbus had been less persevering, the Western Continent might not yet have been discovered.

15. By the enterprising merchants of Venice, the first bank was established.

16. Although surrounded by comforts and luxuries, we may be unhappy.

17. Vasco de Gama, a Portuguese navigator, in 1497, discovered the passage to India around the Cape of Good Hope.

18. The Saxons reduced the greater part of Britain under their sway.

19. Herod was carried to his sepulchre on a bier of gold.

20. With a single stroke of his paw, a lion can break the back of a horse.

LESSON XLV.

VARIETY OF EXPRESSION.

THERE are a number of ways of altering the construction of a sentence, so as to insure variety of expression. To what sentences does the first of these apply?

The first method that we shall consider, applies to sentences that contain a subject, a transitive verb, and an object; as, " Cæsar conquered Pompey."

How may the construction be altered, without changing the meaning?

By making the object the subject, altering the form of the verb, and introducing the subject after the preposition *by*. The sentence given above, altered thus, would read, " Pompey was conquered by Cæsar."

EXERCISE.

Alter the following sentences in the manner described above, being careful to have them retain the same meaning :—

EXAMPLE. Virtue alone produces happiness.

All who know you will admire and respect you.

Altered. Happiness is produced by virtue alone.

You will be admired and respected by all who know you.

1. The ancient Egyptians embalmed the bodies of the dead.

2. Sir Isaac Newton discovered the attraction of gravitation.

3. A courtier of Charles VI. of France invented cards, to amuse the king during his hours of melancholy.

4. Integrity secures the esteem of the world.

5. If the British had subdued our forefathers, we would now be under the dominion of a king.

6. Astronomers calculate eclipses with wonderful precision.

7. Government honored this able statesman with a pension for life.

8. The Chinese may have used gunpowder ages ago.

9. An agent will furnish visitors with maps of the grounds.

10. The cackling of a flock of geese prevented Brennus from taking the citadel of Rome.

11. What great effects may trifling causes produce!

12. An irresistible charge on the part of Murat's gallant cavalry, decided the victory.

13. Two ruffians have attacked and killed an unarmed traveller.

14. A strict government will enforce the laws.

15. Mersennus says that a little child, with a ma-

chine composed of a hundred double pulleys, might move the earth itself.

16. Whatever man has done, man may again do.

17. Perseverance will overcome every obstacle.

18. The greatest minds have admired Milton's "Paradise Lost".

19. During the tenth and the eleventh century, the monarchs of Europe persecuted the Jews with unrelenting cruelty.

20. The bayonet is so called from the inhabitants of Bayonne, who invented it.

LESSON XLVI.

VARIETY OF EXPRESSION.

Is there any other method of obtaining variety of expression, besides the one described in the last lesson?

There is.

To what sentences does it apply?

To sentences in which there are two or more verbs, or two or more clauses, connected by the conjunction *and;* as, " Charles took me aside, and thus addressed me."

How may the construction of such sentences be altered?

By changing one of the verbs (usually the first) into a participle, and leaving out the conjunction *and;* as, " Charles, having taken me aside, thus addressed me."

EXERCISE.

Alter the following sentences in the manner described above; the verb that is to be changed to a participle, is printed in italics :—

EXAMPLE. The wind *was* fair, and we started on our voyage.

The enemy *landed*, and made instant preparation for a march to the capital.

Altered. The wind *being* fair, we started on our voyage.

The enemy, *having landed*, made instant preparation for a march to the capital.

1. The door *was opened*, and a terrible spectacle presented itself to my eyes.

2. Columbus *was convinced* that the world was round, and resolved to test his theory by experiment.

3. The battle *was finished*, and the enemy fell back to the river.

4. Hendrik Hudson *ascended* the river which now bears his name, and founded the city of Albany.

5. The soil of England *is cultivated* with great care, and the harvests are usually abundant.

6. Youth *is* the season of improvement; do not lose one of its precious moments.

7. The trumpet *sounded*, and the combatants charged.

8. My horse *threw* me and *ran* away, and I was obliged to pursue the rest of my journey on foot.

9. The Romans *had conquered* all their enemies, and were, at the time of our Saviour's appearance, masters of the world.

10. The door of the cage *was left* open, and my favorite bird escaped.

11. Hyenas *are* often *driven* to extremity by hunger, and enter church-yards, and *dig* up the bodies of the dead, and feed upon them.

12. His faithful page saw the deadly shaft, and *rushed* before his master, and received it in his own body.

13. Man *rebelled* against his Maker, and sin at once entered the world.

14. Napoleon *was* safely *disposed of* in St. Helena, and ended, on that little island, his tumultuous life.

15. Mungo Park *was filled* with the spirit of discovery, and, at the risk of his life, penetrated the inhospitable regions of Africa.

16. The hardy adventurers *threw* themselves on the ground, and gave thanks to God for the successful issue of their enterprise.

LESSON XLVII.

SYNONYMES.

WHEN is one word said to be the *Synonyme* of another?

A word is said to be the Synonyme of another word, when it means nearly the same thing.

Give an example.

Enough and *sufficient* are synonymes, because they mean nearly the same thing.

Do synonymes convey *precisely* the same idea?

Not often; but they mean *nearly* the same thing.

If you wish to find the synonyme of a word, what book will assist you?

The dictionary.

May a word have more than one synonyme?

Yes, some words have a number of synonymes; thus, *reflect, reckon, deem, suppose, ponder, consider, conclude, judge,* are all synonymes of the word *think.*

Do you mean that, wherever *think* is used, any of these words may be substituted for it without altering the meaning?

No; but *sometimes* they may be substituted for it, without any change in the meaning.

EXERCISE.

Write out the synonymes of the following words; the more you can find, the better your exercise will be. When you are in any difficulty, have recourse to your dictionary.

MODEL. Changeable. Intend.

Synonymes. Variable, fickle, inconstant. Design, purpose, mean.

Color	hinder,	grateful,	bravery,	attack,
path	possess,	powerful,	burden,	divide,
vice	protect,	large,	haste,	use,
prize,	shine,	chief,	industry,	throw,
tidings,	abandon,	sick,	room,	weighty,
tumult,	destroy,	fruitful,	house,	idle,
fear,	forest,	careless,	struggle,	conquer.

LESSON XLVIII.

EXERCISE.

WRITE out and punctuate the following sentences, substituting for each word in italics its synonyme, so that the meaning of the sentence may not be altered:—

MODEL. I am *monarch* of all I *survey*.

I am *lord* of all I *behold*.

1. In Egypt the Nile *annually overflows* the country and thereby *renders* it *fertile*

5

2. In many of the West India islands the *earth* is so *productive* and *requires* so little *cultivation* that *plants* may be said to grow spontaneously

3. It is *reported* of the Emperor Titus that when any one spoke ill of him he was *wont* to say that if the statements were false they would not *injure* him and that if they were true he had more *reason* to be *angry* with himself than with the *narrator*

4. King James of England on one occasion went out of his way to hear a *noted preacher* The *clergyman seeing* the *king* enter departed from the train of his *discourse* and forcibly *portrayed* the *sin* of profane swearing for which James was notorious When he had *concluded* the *monarch* thanked him for his *sermon* but *asked* what connection there was between swearing and his text The *minister immediately answered* Since your majesty *deigned* to come out of your way to meet me I could *hardly* do less than go out of my way to meet you

5. The enemies' *horsemen* were coming up at a *rapid* pace and I was *obliged* to *abandon* my *comrade* to his fate

6. *Indolence* is the *cause* of many evils

7. Wealth is *desired* by all but it is accompanied by many *troubles*

8. Augurelli a *celebrated* Italian *gave* much of his attention to alchemy He was convinced that any metal could be *converted* into gold only one thing *bothered* him and that was to *find out* the way Having *composed* a book on this subject he dedicated it to Pope Leo X *anticipating* a *rich* present in return He was *quite* surprised shortly afterward to *receive* from his Holiness a purse and a letter informing him that *as* he could make gold he *needed* only a purse to put it in

LESSON XLIX.

CIRCUMLOCUTION.

WHAT is Circumlocution?

Circumlocution is the use of two or more words to express the meaning of one ; thus, for *mankind* we may say *the race of men, the human race.*

EXERCISE.

Express the following single words, and such words in the sentences as are in italics, by a circumlocution :—

MODEL.   A *sailor.*

The moon is *shining.*

By Circumlocution.   *One who spends his life upon the ocean.*

The moon is *shedding her light around.*

1. Death.   Heaven.   Astronomy.   A king.   Youth. Benevolence.   A city.   Agriculture.   The sun.   A guardian.   Geography.   Women.   Dishonesty.   Industry.   Autumn.   Children.   Night.   A pronoun.

2. My brother *is dead.*

3. *The poor* are often happier than the rich.

4. Beware of *avarice.*

5. *Virtue* is a source of happiness.

6. The sky is *cloudy.*

7. *Suicide* is a great crime.

8. *The sea is rough.*

9. He *is insensible.*

10. Your cousin *was working.*

LESSON L.

ANALYSIS OF COMPOUND SENTENCES.

WHAT is a Simple Sentence?

A **Simple Sentence** is one that contains but one subject and one predicate; as, "*Friendship adds to our joys.*"

What is a Compound Sentence?

A **Compound Sentence** is one that is composed of two or more simple sentences; as, "*Friendship adds to our joys, and diminishes our sorrows.*"

What is meant by analyzing compound sentences?

Separating them into the simple sentences of which they are composed.

Analyze the compound sentence given above.

Friendship adds to our joys. Friendship diminishes our sorrows.

What word was used in the compound sentence to connect the two simple sentences?

The conjunction *and.*

Is any other part of speech, besides the conjunction, used for this purpose?

Yes, the relative pronoun is often used; as, "*Modesty, which is one of the most attractive virtues, is a great preservative against vice.*"

Analyze the compound sentence just given.

Modesty is one of the most attractive virtues. Modesty is a great preservative against vice.

In analyzing a compound sentence, what must we do?

We must remove the connecting word, if there be any, and repeat, in each simple sentence, such words as may be necessary to complete the sense.

Analyze the following compound sentences :—

EXAMPLE. Mahomet, the founder of the Mahometan religion, did not hesitate to work with his own hands; he kindled his own fire, swept his room, made his bed, milked his ewes and camels, mended his stockings, and scoured his sword.

Simple Sentences. Mahomet was the founder of the Mahometan religion.

Mahomet did not hesitate to work with his own hands.

Mahomet kindled his own fire.

Mahomet swept his own room.

Mahomet made his own bed.

Mahomet milked his own ewes and camels.

Mahomet mended his own stockings.

Mahomet scoured his own sword.

1. Aristarchus of Samos, who was a little wiser than his contemporaries, was the first to assert that the earth moved.

2. Whereupon he was accused, before the court of Areopagus, of violating morality and introducing inn - vations in religion.

3. Aristotle, one of the most sensible of the ancient philosophers, thought that the earth was shaped like a timbrel.

5. Without books, justice is dormant, philosophy lame, letters are dumb, and all things are involved in darkness.

5. Æsop and Terence, those admirable writers, were slaves.

6. The sun shines by day, and the moon by night.

7. Modern times, with all their boasted progress,

have never produced as strong a man as Samson, as meek a man as Moses, or as wise a man as Solomon.

8. A simpleton fancied, in a dream, that he had trodden on a nail, and, on waking, bound up his foot.

9. Another simpleton, learning the cause, said: "I do not pity you, for why do you sleep without sandals?"

10. Cæsar crossed the Rubicon, overran Italy, entered Rome, and seized upon the public treasury.

LESSON LI.

SYNTHESIS OF SIMPLE SENTENCES.

WHAT is the opposite of analysis?

Synthesis.

What is meant by the Synthesis of simple sentences?

The union of two or more simple sentences in such a way as to form one compound sentence.

In such a union, what changes are necessary?

The words that are repeated in the simple sentences must be omitted, and the proper connective (a conjunction or a relative pronoun) inserted.

EXERCISE.

Unite the simple sentences given in each paragraph below, into one compound sentence:—

EXAMPLE. The White Sea is so called on account of its color. The White Sea is constantly frozen over. The White Sea is covered with snow.

Compound Sentence. The White Sea is so called on account of its color, as it is constantly frozen over and covered with snow.

1. I love to contemplate the wonders of the earth. I love to reflect on the glory of the Creator.

2. Beware of avarice. Avarice is incompatible with reason. Avarice has ruined the souls of myriads.

3. Let your pleasure be moderate. Let your pleasure be seasonable. Let your pleasure be innocent. Let your pleasure be becoming.

4. Without modesty, beauty is ungraceful. Without modesty, learning is unattractive. Without modesty, wit is disgusting.

5. Wealth is much sought after. Wealth brings with it many troubles.

6. In Spitzbergen there is a long day of six months. In Spitzbergen there is a long night of six months.

7. Charlemagne was the most powerful monarch of his age. Charlemagne added much to his glory by inviting learned men to his court. Charlemagne added much to his glory by inviting scientific men to his court.

8. Black pepper is produced in Java. Black pepper is produced in Sumatra. Black pepper grows upon a vine. The vine resembles our grape-vine.

9. Plato was told that some enemies had spoken ill of him. Plato said, "It matters not." Plato said, "I will endeavor so to live that no one shall believe them."

10. Xerxes resolved to invade Greece. Xerxes raised an army. The army consisted of two million of men. This was the greatest force that was ever brought into the field.

11. The hills are covered with a carpet of green. The meadows are covered with a carpet of green.

12. Life is short. Life is unsatisfactory. Life is uncertain.

LESSON LII.

STYLE.

WHAT is Style?

Style is the particular manner in which a writer or speaker expresses his thoughts by words.

From what is the word *style* derived?

From the Latin word *stylus,* a pointed steel instrument which the Romans used in writing upon their waxen tablets.

Do the styles of most writers differ?

They do; no two writers are likely to express the same idea in precisely the same manner.

What are the principal kinds of style?

The Simple, the Florid, the Nervous, the Concise, the Diffuse.

What is meant by Simple Style? *

Simple Style is that in which the thoughts are expressed in a natural manner, without any attempt at effect.

What is meant by Florid Style?

Florid Style is that in which there is a great deal of ornament.

What is meant by Nervous Style?

Nervous Style is that in which forcible sentences are employed, and which makes a strong impression on the reader or hearer.

What is meant by Concise Style?

Concise Style is that in which the thoughts are expressed in very few words.

---

* Examples of the different kinds of style will be found in the Exercise at the end of this Lesson.

What is meant by Diffuse Style?

Diffuse Style is that of a writer or speaker who enlarges on his thoughts, and uses many words to express them.

To what should the style of an author always be suited?

To the subject he is treating.

There are certain properties which the style of every good writer must possess; what are these?

Purity, Propriety, Precision, Clearness, Strength, and Harmony.

EXERCISE.

Copy and punctuate the following extracts, which are examples of the different kinds of style :—

Simple Style.

" Sweet was the sound, when oft at evening's close
Up yonder hill the village murmur rose,
There as I passed with careless steps and slow,
The mingled notes came softened from below,
The swain responsive as the milk-maid sung,
The sober herd that lowed to meet their young
The noisy geese that gabbled o'er the pool
The playful children just let loose from school
The watch-dog's voice that bayed the whispering wind
And the loud laugh that spoke the vacant mind
These all in sweet confusion sought the shade
And filled each pause the nightingale had made "

Florid Style. " His charmed numbers flow on like the free current of a melodious stream whose associations are with the sunbeams and the shadows. The leafy boughs the song of the forest birds the dew upon the flowery bank and all things sweet and genial and delightful whose influence is around us in our happiest moments, and whose essence is the wealth that lies hoarded in the treasury of nature "

Nervous Style.

"Vengeance calls you quick be ready
Rouse ye in the name of God
Onward onward strong and steady
Dash to earth the oppressor's rod
Vengeance calls ye brave ye brave
Rise and spurn the name of slave."

Concise Style.

" He touched his harp, and nations heard entranced
As some vast river of unfailing source
Rapid exhaustless deep his numbers flowed
And oped new fountains in the human heart
*   *   *   With Nature's self,
He seemed an old acquaintance, free to jest
At will with all her glorious majesty,
He laid his hand upon the ocean's mane
And played familiar with his hoary locks
Stood on the Alps stood on the Apennines
And with the thunder talked as friend to friend
Suns moons and stars and clouds his sisters were
Rocks mountains meteors seas and winds and storms
His brothers younger brothers whom he scarce
As equals deemed "

Diffuse Style. "The fame of his discovery had resounded throughout the nation and as the route of Columbus lay through several of the finest and most populous provinces of Spain, his journey appeared like the progress of a sovereign. Wherever he passed the surrounding country poured forth its inhabitants who lined the roads and thronged the villages .In the large towns the streets, windows, and balconies, were filled with eager spectators, who rent the air with acclamations. His journey was continually impeded, by the multitude, pressing to gain a sight of him, and of the Indians, who were regarded with, as much admiration, as if they had been natives of another planet. It was impossible to satisfy the craving curiosity, which assailed himself, and his attendants, at every stage with innumerable questions, popular rumor, as usual had exaggerated the truth, and had filled, the newly found country, with all kinds of wonders."

LESSON LIII.

PURITY.

WHAT is the first essential property of a good style?

Purity.

In what does Purity consist?

Purity of style consists in the use of such words and modes of expression as are warranted by good authority.

What is meant by " good authority"?

The usage of the best writers and speakers.

How many rules must be observed, to insure purity of style?

Three :—

I. Do not use foreign words or modes of construction, when there are pure English ones that are just as expressive.

II. Do not use obsolete words, or such as have fallen into disuse.

III. Avoid words that are not authorized by good writers.

Mention some of the foreign words that are often introduced by writers who violate the first rule relating to purity, and the corresponding English words that should be used instead of them.

Hauteur, haughtiness.   *Émeute*, disturbance.
Délicatesse, delicacy.   *Bagatelle*, trifle.
Politesse, politeness.   *N'importe*, no matter.
À propos, appropriate.   *Nous verrons*, we shall see.

Mention some obsolete words, and what it is proper to use instead of them at the present day.

Let, hinder.   *Irks*, wearies.
Behest, command.   *Wot*, know.
Quoth, said.   *Wist*, knew.
Erst, formerly.   *Sith*, since.

EXERCISE.

Correct the following sentences, so that they may contain no violation of the rules for purity :—

EXAMPLE.   I can not believe it, but *nous verrons.*
He *repented him* of his fault.

Corrected.   I can not believe it, but *we shall see.*
He *repented* of his fault.

1. His manners were not marked by *politesse*, but by an offensive *hauteur.*

2. I have been disappointed, but *n'importe.*

3. Fearing that they might become involved in the *émeute*, they remained in the house.

4. My friend made some remarks quite *à propos* to the occasion.

5. The fleeting joys of this world are but *bagatelles.*

6. I can go where *likes me* best.

7. Thy voice we hear, and thy *behests* obey.

8. " Come," *quoth* he, " lay aside thine armor."

9. I *wot* not who it was.

10. *It irks me* to see such obstinacy.

11. The nobles of England dwelt *erst* in strongly-fortified castles.

12. Having nothing to do, he employed his time in *stroaming* about the fields.

13. Thy speech *bewrayeth* thee.

14. He comes to the city *dailily*.

15. I admire his *délicatesse* and *candidness*.

16. Her *amiableness* endears her to all her friends.

17. His severe administration of the laws rendered him very *impopular*.

18. St. Augustine lived *godlily*.

19. I could not account for his *merriness*.

20. Damp weather is very *unagreeable*.

LESSON LIV.

PROPRIETY.

WHAT is the second essential property of a good style?

Propriety.

In what does Propriety consist?

Propriety consists in the selection of such words as the best usage has appropriated to the ideas intended to be expressed.

To insure propriety, what kind of expressions must we be careful to avoid?

Low and vulgar expressions, which are often used in conversation, but are not sufficiently dignified to be admitted into composition.

The words in italics in the following sentences are to be corrected, so that there may be no violation of propriety :—

EXAMPLE.   My father *has got the blues.*
Corrected.   My father *is in low spirits.*

1. I saw *with half an eye* that it was necessary for me to observe great caution.

2. As the noise disturbed me, I told him to *hold his tongue.*

3. They *have got* the small-pox.

4. Having run up to see what *the matter was,* I became involved among the rioters, and, before I could extricate myself, came near *getting my head broken.*

5. He is not *a bit* better than he ought to be.

6. My cousin is *mad at* me.

7. He saw the horses dashing toward him *full split,* and, making a desperate leap, escaped *by the skin of his teeth.*

8. Every one *sets store by* a good boy.

9. I would *as lief* live in America as in Europe.

10. James is *something of a scholar.*

11. She is *in a bad fix.*

12. John *turns up his nose at* every thing.

13. If a clerk *cheat,* he will soon be *turned out of his situation.*

14. He tries to *curry favor with* his superiors.

15. Their coming in *turned every thing topsy-turvy.*

16. We *have a great mind* to go to Harlem to-morrow.

17. She is a very *stingy* woman.

LESSON LV.

PRECISION.

WHAT is the third essential property of a good style?

Precision.

In what does Precision consist?

Precision consists in the use of such words as exactly express the idea intended to be conveyed.

In what is precision most frequently violated?

In the use of words which are generally considered synonymous, but which do not convey the same meaning.

Give an example.

Courage and *fortitude* are generally thought to mean the same thing; but their exact significations are widely different. *Courage* is shown in braving danger; *fortitude*, in supporting pain. In such a sentence as this, "John displayed great *courage*, while undergoing the operation," precision is violated. The word *courage* is misused, and the sentence should be, "John displayed great *fortitue* while undergoing the operation."

Mention some other words that are often used as synonymous.

Discovery and *invention; effect* and *influence; custom* and *habit; vacant* and *empty; great* and *big.*

In what other way is precision often violated?

By substituting for the proper word, another word formed from the same primitive, but which ought to be differently applied; as, *observation* for *observance, conscience* for *consciousness.*

Give an example.

"*Negligence* of duty often produces misery." There is a violation of precision in the use of *negligence* for *neglect*. The sentence should read thus: "*Neglect* of duty often produces misery."

EXERCISE.

The words in italics, in the following sentences, are to be altered, so that there may be no violation of precision. Examples are given above.

1. Columbus *invented* America. Newton *invented* the attraction of gravitation.

2. The *discovery* of steamboats produced a most beneficial *influence* on the commerce of the whole world.

3. The cavalry charged with their accustomed *fortitude*.

4. Smoking is a bad *custom*.

5. James endured the pain with a great deal of *courage*.

6. The house was closed, and we naturally supposed it to be *empty*.

7. All the furniture had been removed; every room was *vacant*.

8. He is a very talented and studious boy, and will, no doubt, become a *big* man.

9. A frog once swelled herself out, till she thought herself *greater* than an ox.

10. *Conscience* of integrity supports the *misfortunate*.

11. The *observation* of the Sabbath is a distinguishing mark of Christian nations.

12. The bird escaped through her *neglect*.

13. The bird died through her *negligence*.

14. The farmers of Ohio pay great attention to the *culture* of corn.

15. *Proposals* were then made by the opposite party, which we were invited to discuss with their agent.

16. The prince next made *propositions* of marriage to the daughter of the King of Denmark.

17. *Intoleration* in religion has been the cause of much suffering.

18. The magistrate, having heard the prisoner's story, expressed his *disbelief* of every word he had uttered.

LESSON LVI.

CLEARNESS.

What is the fourth essential property of a good style?

Clearness.

In what does Clearness consist?

Clearness consists in such a use and arrangement of words and clauses as at once distinctly indicate the meaning of the writer or speaker.

What is the opposite of clearness?

Obscurity.

What are the most frequent causes of obscurity?

The use of ambiguous or equivocal words, and the improper arrangement of words or clauses.

Repeat the three rules for promoting clearness, that relate to the use of words.

Rule I. Avoid ambiguous expressions.

Rule II. Do not make the same pronoun refer to different objects in the same sentence.

Rule III. Insert words that are wanting, when they cannot not readily be supplied by the mind.

Correct the following sentences, so that they may contain no violation of Rules I., II., and III., for the promotion of clearness :—

EXAMPLE.   1. The *reproof* of the erring is a duty.

2. Charles promised *his* father that he would never forget *his* advice.

3. We love who flatter us.

Corrected. The first sentence is ambiguous; it may mean either that *it is the duty of the erring to reprove others,* or that *it is the duty of others to reprove the erring.* We will therefore alter it thus :—

1. To reprove the erring is a duty.

The second sentence contains a violation of Rule II., because the first *his* refers to *Charles,* while the second refers to *father.* This fault may be corrected by making the sentence read thus :—

2. Charles promised his father, "I will never forget thy advice."

In the third sentence, the word that is omitted can not readily be supplied by the mind, and we must therefore insert it :—

3. We love *those* who flatter us.

1. We speak that we know.

2. We dislike who dislike us.

3. *My beating* did him good.   (*Ambiguous, because it may mean either the beating I gave him, or the beating he gave me.*)

4. *The love of a parent* is a natural feeling.

5. *Our rebuke* had its intended effect.

6. *The officer's instructions* were plain.

7. We are naturally inclined to praise who praise us.

8. Who is most industrious is most happy.

9. There were several of the crew died on the passage.

10. The worst can be said of him is, that he is some-times inattentive.

11. There are many men waste their lives in idleness.

12. Galileo was led to invent the pendulum, by a chandelier he frequently observed swinging to and fro in the cathedral of Florence.

13. The farmer went to *his* neighbor, and told him that *his* cattle were in *his* field.

14. Damon told the king that *he* would not comply with *his* demands.

15. *The nobleman's summons* was unheeded.

16. The clerk told *his* employer, whatever *he* did, *he* could not please *him*.

17. There was one man was struck by the ball.

18. It was the bodies of distinguished persons only, were embalmed by the ancient Egyptians.

LESSON LVII.

CLEARNESS.

In what does clearness consist?

What is the opposite of clearness?

Repeat the three rules for promoting clearness, that relate to the use of words.

Repeat the rule that relates to the arrangement of words and clauses.

Place words and clauses as near as possible to the words to which they relate.

What words are most frequently misplaced?

Adverbs; particularly *only* and *not only*.

What is the effect of their being misplaced?

They are thereby made to modify a different

word from the one intended, and the whole mean-ing of the sentence is changed.

Give an example.

"*He not only owns a house, but also a large farm.*" *Not only*, as it now stands, modifies the verb *owns*, and from the beginning of the sentence one would suppose that another verb was to follow —that he not only *owns* the house, but *lives* in it, or something of that kind. Whereas *not only* is intended to modify *house*, and it should be placed as near it as possible ; thus, "*He owns not only a house, but also a large farm.*"

How should a relative clause be placed ?

Immediately after its antecedent.

That you may accomplish this, how must you alter the follow-ing sentence, in which, it will be seen, another noun stands be-tween the antecedent and the relative clause ? "*A servant will obey a master's orders, that he loves.*"

Change *master's* to *of a master*, and place *or-ders* before it ; thus, "A servant will obey the orders of a master that he loves." We thus bring the relative clause immediately after the antece-dent, *master.*

Alter in this way the following sentences, so that the relative clause may immediately follow its antecedent : ___

1. The mariner's compass was Gioia's invention, a celebrated mathematician of Naples.

2. Have you read Tasso's work, the immortal Italian poet?

EXERCISE.

Arrange the words and clauses in the following sentences in such a way that there may be no vio—lation of the last rule for promoting clearness:___

EXAMPLE. 1. The mate saved a man from drowning, who was an excellent swimmer.

2. The man was digging a well, with a Roman nose.

3. It is my friend's son, whom I love so well.

4. We should not only love our relatives, but our friends also.

Properly Arranged. 1. The mate, who was an excellent swimmer, saved a man from drowning.

2. The man with a Roman nose, was digging a well.

3. It is the son of my friend, whom I love so well.

4. We should love, not only our relatives, but our friends also.

1. The Romans now proclaimed war against the Parthians, who had conquered all the rest of the world.

2. Glass windows were first used in England, A. D. 674, as we learn from Bede's works, the venerable historian.

3. Many of the best English authors flourished in Queen Elizabeth's reign, who patronized not only literary men, but herself p etended to be an author

4. The lady was sewing with sore eyes.

5. Boston was Franklin's birthplace, the celebrated American philosopher, who not only won the respect of his own country, but of all Europe.

6. Washington not only won the respect, but the love, of all true Americans.

7. Dr. Johnson was once arrested for a debt of five guineas, the author of the dictionary.

8. Sir Isaac Newton's great mind was principally directed to mathematics.

9. The ungenerous person only thinks of himself.

10. The horse is ploughing with a switch tail.

11. This work, being afflicted with the rheumatism, I am obliged at present to discontinue.

12. I was afraid to ride a horse, having a disease of the heart.

13. The disorderly persons were removed from the room, in consequence of being intoxicated, by the assistance of several gentlemen present.

14. The Emperor Augustus was a patron of learned men, at least.

15. So utterly was Carthage destroyed, that we are unable to point out the place where it stood at the present day.

16. The steamer from Liverpool is soon expected to arrive.

LESSON LVIII.

STRENGTH.

WHAT is the fifth essential property of a good style?

Strength.

In what does Strength consist?

Strength consists in such a use and arrangement of words as make a deep impression on the mind of the reader or hearer.

Would strength be a characteristic of the following sentence? —" *The general ordered the captain to order the soldiers to observe good order.*"

No.

What makes it weak?

The repetition of the word *order*.

What is this fault in writing called?

Tautology.

What is Tautology?

Tautology is the repetition of the same, or a similar, word in a sentence.

How may tautology be corrected?

By substituting a synonyme for the word repeated.

What is a synonyme? (See Lesson XLVII.)

Correct in this way the sentence given above.

" *The general* directed *the captain to* command *the soldiers to observe good order.*"

In the sentence, "*We looked out of the window, and took a view,*" does the clause, *took a view,* add any thing to the meaning?

It does not.

What, then, is its effect on the sentence?

It weakens the sentence.

What is this fault called?

Redundancy.

What is Redundancy?

Redundancy is the repetition of an idea in the same sentence.

How may redundancy be corrected?

By leaving out the superfluous word or clause.

Correct in this way the sentence given above.

" *We looked out of the window.*"

What two short rules will conduce much to strength of style?

Rule I. Avoid tautology.

Rule II. Avoid redundancy.

EXERCISE.

Correct the tautology and redundancy in the following sentences :—

EXAMPLE. 1. He *said* that his father *said* that he would not leave the city.

2. Washington was a *good* and *excellent* man.

Corrected. 1. He *stated* that his father said that he would not leave the city.

2. Washington was an excellent man.

1. The sexton told the minister that he had tolled the bell for an hour.

2. He went to Baltimore by steamboat, and thence went to Philadelphia by railroad.

3. Mahomet was distinguished by the dignity and majesty of his person.

4. She is so lovely a woman that no one can help loving her.

5. The ancient Egyptians used to use myrrh, spices, and nitre, for embalming the dead bodies of the deceased.

6. Sit down, and take a seat.

7. The brilliant brightness of the sun makes all na-ture look lively and animated.

8. The children are playing in the umbrageous shadow of a shady oak.

9. They returned back again to the same place from whence they came.

10. While travelling through Russia, we met a traveller, who, in seven days, had travelled over a thousand miles.

11. Generals are generally men of decision and energy.

12. No Christian will revenge himself on his enemies, and take vengeance on his foes.

13. Charlemagne found that his subjects were very ignorant, and therefore founded several seminaries of learning; but all his attempts and efforts were insufficient and unable to enlighten the darkness of his age.

14. No learning is generally so dearly bought, or so valuable when it is bought, as the learning that we learn in the school of experience.

LESSON LIX.

STRENGTH.

In what does strength consist?

What is tautology?

What is redundancy?

Repeat the two short rules for promoting strength.

Give three more rules, the observance of which will conduce much to strength of style.

Rule III. Do not use the conjunction *and* too much, or let it commence a sentence.

Rule IV. Do not end a sentence with a preposition, an unimportant word, or a succession of short words.

Rule V. When there are several similar dependent clauses, as a general thing, place the longest last, and do not let a weaker assertion follow a stronger.

EXERCISE.

Correct the following sentences, so that there may be no violation of the rules just given :-

EXAMPLE. 1. Idleness, and luxury, and pleasure, destroy many a youth.

2. Ingratitude is a crime that I can not accuse myself of.

3. Catiline plunged into every species of iniquity, and left the path of virtue.

Corrected. 1. Idleness, luxury, and pleasure, destroy many a youth.

2. Ingratitude is a crime of which I can not accuse myself.

3. Catiline left the path of virtue, and plunged into every species of iniquity.

1. Charlemagne was a successful warrior, and a sound statesman, and an able monarch.

2. And he evinced incredible activity; he superintended the public improvements, and managed the affairs of the kingdom, and still found time to foster literature and the arts.

3. He is one that I can not depend on.

4. Galileo made many discoveries in astronomy, but he was imprisoned on account of them.

5. Charity ought to exert an influence over all our actions, and regulate our speech.

6. The faith which Mahomet professed, and which he was the author of, soon spread over Arabia, and Turkey, and the northern part of Africa.

7. His conduct was disgraceful; it was unbecoming.

8. There are many mysteries which we can not understand, yet which we must believe in.

9. His assistance I am sure of.

10. Robert Burns, although originally a poor ploughman, was one that men of letters were glad to be acquainted with, and associate with.

11. When one is out of health, life becomes a burden, and there is no pleasure in it.

12. His gross excesses, and indulgence in pleasure, cut him off at an early age.

LESSON LX.

HARMONY.

WHAT is the sixth essential property of a good style?

Harmony.

In what does Harmony consist?

Harmony consists in that smooth and easy flow which pleases the ear.

What words are, for the most part, inharmonious?

1. Such as are derived from long compound words; as, *sobermindedness, shamefacedness.*

2. Such as contain a great number of consonants; as, *phthisic, asthma.*

3. Such as are composed of a number of short syllables, with the accent on or near the first; as, *primarily, temporarily.*

What combination of words is found to be inharmonious?

A succession of words of the same length. Thus, "*no kind of joy can long please us,*" is by no means as harmonious as, "*no* species *of joy can long* delight *us*".

What other combination of words should be avoided?

A succession of words that resemble each other in the sound of any of their syllables. Thus, "*a fair fairy*," "*a mild child*," are less harmonious than "*a* handsome *fairy*," "*a* gentle *child*".

As to the general arrangement of words and clauses, what is the best guide?

The ear.

What kind of style is generally harmonious?

A strong style.

EXERCISE.

Correct the following sentences in such a way that their harmony may be increased. When any particular word causes the want of harmony, it is in italics.

EXAMPLE.   1. *Shamefacedness* has been a characteristic of many distinguished men.

2. He went to Rome with a friend.*

3. This I consider to be a true *union*.

Corrected.   1. *Bashfulness* has been a characteristic of many distinguished men.

2. He *proceeded* to Rome with a friend.

3. This I consider to be a true *friendship*.

1. All rich men have a sly way of jesting, which would make no great show were they not rich men.*

2. Reason seldom governs passion, but passion often governs reason.†

3. The slow horse goes not to the race till it is done.*

4. Camoens lived *temporarily* in the East Indies.

5. *Many men* disregard their duty.

6. *In In*dia, *in*nocent *in*fants are thrown into the Ganges.

7. Peace should be sought for by us and by all.*

8. The *peaceableness* of his disposition gained him many friends.

9. He kept *wriggling* in a very uneasy manner.

10. Pope was accustomed to speak *derogatorily* of his friends.

11. Her cheerful temper and pleasant humor procured her general esteem.†

12. All that afflicts us here will pass away soon.

13. The seas shall waste, and rocks shall fall to dust.

14. The *favorableness* with which the Waverley novels were received, is almost incredible.

---

* Too many words of one syllable.
† Too many words of two syllables.

15. Seizing the first oppor*tunity*, I impor*tuned* him for his assistance.

16. The *homely home* of poverty is often the seat of greater happiness than the grandest mansion.

17. It is *poss*ible to *poss*ess wisdom without learning.

18. Some regard *sobermindedness* as essential to a good character.

19. He re*pressed* the ex*pression* which was on his lips.

20. He conducted the business *unsatisfactorily.*

LESSON LXI.

UNITY.

WHAT does every sentence contain?

One leading thought, or proposition.

May it not contain more than one proposition?

It may, if they are intimately connected with the leading one, and properly introduced.

What do you mean by *properly introduced?*

Introduced without too frequent a change of subject.

Give an example.

"*My friends turned back, after we reached the vessel, on board of which I was received with kindness by the passengers, who vied with each other in showing me attention.*" In this sentence we have no less than four subjects, *friends, we, I, who;* and the frequent change produces great confusion in the mind.

What is the fault in this sentence called?

A violation of Unity.

In what does Unity consist?

Unity consists in the restriction of a sentence to one leading proposition, modified only by such kindred ideas as are closely connected with it.

Give an example of a sentence in which unity is violated by joining two propositions that have no connection.

"*Archbishop Tillotson died in this year. He was exceedingly beloved by King William and Queen Mary, who nominated Dr. Tennison, bishop of Lincoln, to succeed him.*" In the last sentence there is a gross violation of unity, in connecting the nomination of Dr. Tennison with the great love entertained by the king and queen for Archbishop Tillotson.

Give three rules that will conduce to the preservation of unity.

Rule I. Introduce as few subjects as possible into a sentence.

Rule II. Do not crowd into one sentence things that have no connection.

Rule III. Avoid the introduction of long parentheses.

Are parentheses as much used as they formerly were?

No; good writers of the present day, for the most part, avoid them altogether.

Are all parentheses inadmissible?

No; short ones, when properly introduced, may often be used with advantage; but in long and complicated ones the mind is distracted from the leading proposition, and obscurity and weakness ensue.

When a violation of unity occurs, how are we to correct it?

I. If it proceeds from a variety of subjects, get

rid of some of them, by adopting participial clauses, or a different form of the verb.

Thus, the first example of a violation of unity given above, may be corrected as follows:—" *My friends* having turned *back after we reached the vessel, the passengers received me on board with kindness, and vied with each other in showing me attention.*" The sentence, as thus corrected, has but two subjects, *we* and *passengers.*

II. If it proceeds from the introduction of two or more unconnected propositions, or of a parenthesis, we must separate the sentence into two or more shorter sentences.

Thus, the second example of a violation of unity given above, may be corrected as follows:—"*Archbishop Tillotson died in this year. He was exceedingly beloved by King William and Queen Mary. Dr. Tennison, bishop of Lincoln, was nominated to succeed him.*"

EXERCISE.

Correct the following sentences, so that they may contain no violation of unity. The pupil will, of course, make such changes in the punctuation as may be required.

Examples of this fault and its correction have been given above.

1. The next lady to whom I was introduced was the Duchess of Devonshire, who received me with great affability, and, no long time afterward, had her neck broken in consequence of being thrown from her carriage.

2. Lord Bacon's maxims are full of philosophy; but he was a very mean man.

3. The bear is capable of strong attachment, and its flesh makes very juicy and excellent food.

4. Father Carli says that the camel, which is the most patient of animals, retains the remembrance of an injury that has been done to it, until an opportunity of revenge occurs.

5. The dog is an animal of wonderful sagacity, and it is used by the Esquimaux for drawing sleds.

6. The quicksilver mines of Idria, in Austria, (which were discovered in 1797, by a peasant, who, catching some water from a spring, found the tub so heavy that he could not move it, and the bottom covered with a shining substance which turned out to be mercury,) yield, every year, between 300,000 and 400,000 pounds of that valuable metal.

7. The trappers of the Rocky Mountains obtain the necessaries of life in exchange for beaver-skins, which are worth from four to eight dollars a pound.

8. The first gold pens (which have now come into use both in this country and in Europe, and which are generally preferred to any other kind) were made in 1836.

LESSON LXII.

A REVIEW.

WHAT is style? (See Lesson LII.) From what is the word *style* derived? What are the principal kinds of style? Describe simple style; florid style; nervous style; concise style; diffuse style.

Mention the six essential properties of a good style.

In what does purity consist? (See Lesson LIII.) What three classes of words do the rules for purity forbid us to use?

In what does propriety consist? (See Lesson LIV.) What kind of expressions does propriety forbid us to use?

In what does precision consist? (See Lesson LV.) In what way is precision often violated? Mention some words that are often used as synonymes, but which really differ in their meaning.

In what does clearness consist? (See Lessons LVI. and LVII.) What is the opposite of clearness? To promote clearness, what words must be avoided? What is the rule with regard to making the same pronoun refer to different objects? When must we insert words that are omitted? How must words and clauses be placed? What words are most frequently misplaced?

In what does strength consist? (See Lessons LVIII. and LIX.) What is tautology? How may it be corrected?

What is redundancy? How may it be corrected?

Repeat the two short rules for the promotion of strength. What rule relates to the conjunction *and?* With what must you be careful not to end a sentence? When you have several similar dependent clauses, which should come last? When you have several assertions, which should come last?

In what does harmony consist? (See Lesson LX.) What three classes of words are, for the most part, inharmonious? What combinations of words are found to be inharmonious? What is the best guide for the general arrangement of words and clauses?

In what does unity consist? (See Lesson LXI.) Repeat the three rules for the preservation of unity.

MISCELLANEOUS EXERCISE.

Punctuate the following sentences, and correct them so that they may contain no violation of the rules for purity, propriety, precision, clearness, strength, harmony, and unity :—

1. In the last Punic war the Romans soon *got the upper hand* of the Carthaginians

2. The earth moves round the sun at a quick rate

3. A French *savant* at a late meeting of the *literati* and scientific men of Paris by a chemical process froze some drops of water in a red-hot cup

4. The sky in New Holland is so singular and so beautiful in appearance that *even* the *writers'* descriptions who have been there can give us no adequate idea respecting it

5. No nation on the earth are so generally cheerful and light-hearted that I have met with as the French

6. He endeavored to *disarm* my fears by ordering the *army* who were all well *armed* to lay aside their *arms*

7. He looked coldly at me *and eyed me sternly*

8. The criminals were next placed *in an en*ormous car

9. We know that it is hard to do right still let us try to do it

10. *Amethyst* means ' that which does not intoxicate' and it was so called because it was a prevalent *doctrine* among the ancients that wine would lose its intoxicating *influence* if drunk from a cup of this precious stone

11. In the middle ages it was a *habit* for pilgrims to flock from all parts of the globe to the tomb of our Saviour

12. There was no crime that Catiline was not guilty *of* He ruined *not only* a great number of young men but attempted to *ruin* his country itself

LESSON LXIII.

DIFFERENT KINDS OF COMPOSITION.—ANALYSIS OF SUBJECTS.

WHAT is Composition?

Composition is the art of expressing one's thoughts by means of written language.

What are the two great divisions under which all compositions may be classed?

Prose and Poetry.

What compositions fall under the head of Prose?

All those in which a natural method of expression and a natural order are employed, without reference to the recurrence of certain sounds, or any exact arrangement of syllables.

What compositions fall under the head of Poetry?

All those in which there is a departure from the natural order, or mode of expression; or in which there is a recurrence of certain sounds, or an exact arrangement of syllables.

Which of these two great divisions shall we now proceed to consider?

Prose.

What are the principal divisions under which the varieties of prose composition may be classed?

There are five leading divisions; viz., Letters, Descriptions, Narrations, Essays, and Argumentative Discourses.*

When a subject has been selected, no matter to which of these divisions your composition is to belong, what is the first thing to be done?

To reflect upon the various branches of the subject, to think what can be said about it, and then proceed to its analysis.

What is meant by the Analysis of a subject?

By the Analysis of a subject is meant the draw-

* *Note to the Teacher.*—The author has deemed it inexpedient to present the formal divisions usually given by rhetoricians. He has selected such as are essential, and seem properly to fall within the province of an elementary work.

ing out of the various heads under which it is intended to treat it.

Will the analysis of all subjects be the same?

No; the heads will depend altogether on the subject.

Suppose " COMMERCE " to be given you as your subject, how would you analyze it?

A proper analysis of " Commerce " would be as follows :—

COMMERCE.

I. DEFINITION.   (What is commerce ?)

II. ORIGIN.   (Under this head state who were the first to engage in commerce; the date; what other nations soon followed in their steps.)

III. HISTORY.   (State how commerce was originally carried on; describe the over-land trade between Europe and the East Indies.)

IV. DISCOVERIES.   (Describe the two important discoveries that were made near the close of the 15th century; viz., the discovery of America by Columbus, and that of a passage to the Indies around the Cape of Good Hope.   Mention their effects on the commerce of the world.)

V. ADVANTAGES.

1. Equalizing the supply of the productions of the earth.

2. Diffusing the blessings of education and civilization.

3. Spreading the truths of Christianity.

When you have a material object to describe, the analysis would be somewhat different. Take, for example, " SHIPS " for your subject, and analyze it.

SHIPS.

I. ORIGIN. (When and by whom were the first ships made?)

II. APPEARANCE. (What was their original form, and what improvements have modern times made in them?)

III. OBJECTS for which they are used.

IV. INVENTIONS that have added to their usefulness. (Particularly the mariners' compass, and its effects.)

V. EFFECTS that ships have produced on mankind.

VI. FEELINGS excited by seeing a ship under full sail.

What heads belong to almost every subject?

Such general heads as Origin, History, Object, Effects, &c.

EXERCISE.

Copy the two analyses given above.

Analyze the following subjects according to the directions and models that have been given, remembering to ponder each subject carefully, and to give under each all the heads that you can think of:—

I. A CITY.	IV. EVENING.
II. SCHOOLS.	V. HOUSES.
III. A RAILROAD.	VI. WINTER.

———

LESSON LXIV.

LETTER-WRITING.

WHAT is the first division belonging to prose composition?

Letters.

What makes this an important branch?

The necessity that exists for all persons, no matter what their business may be, to write letters.

On what subjects are letters most frequently composed?

On the ordinary topics of business or friendship.

Is the form of the letter ever used for other subjects?

Yes, some writers have adopted the letter form in the composition of Philosophical Essays, Novels, Histories, &c.; that is, they have published these productions, with an address to some friend, as if they had really passed as letters.

Would compositions of this kind properly fall under the head of Letters?

No; they should be classed under the division to which they really belong.

What, then, are properly embraced under the head of Letter-Writing, or Epistolary Correspondence, as it is sometimes called?

Letters that are really intended for those to whom they are addressed.

What is the principal requisite of a good letter?

A simple and concise style. There should be no attempt at display.

What is to be avoided?

A tendency to diffuseness, proceeding from a fear that there may not be enough matter to fill the sheet.

Before commencing your letter, what is it best to do?

To think over the various subjects on which it is intended to write, and draw out the heads on a separate piece of paper. In this way repetition will be avoided, and a proper arrangement insured.

What rule is to be observed with regard to commencing a new paragraph, in either a letter or any other piece of composition?

Commence a new paragraph whenever it is necessary to pass from one head of the letter or subject to another.

What is the best method of preserving neatness in a letter or other composition?

Draw two light pencil lines parallel with the left edge of the sheet, the first about half an inch, the second an inch, distant from it. Commence your composition, and each paragraph that follows, on the second or inner line; but carry out the body of the composition to the first or outer marginal line. When you have completed a page, erase the lines neatly with india-rubber.*

Describe the date of a letter.

A letter should always be dated. The date consists of the name of the place, the day of the month, and the year; thus, *Charleston, January* 1, 1869.

Describe the address of a letter.

In the first line of the address, give the name and title of the person to whom the letter is written. On the second line, address a gentleman as " Sir," " Dear Sir," or " My dear Sir "—a married lady as " Madam," " Dear Madam," or " My dear Madam "—according to the degree of intimacy.

How is an unmarried lady best addressed?

In one line; as, " My dear Miss ——".

How should a relative or friend be addressed?

---

* *Note to the Teacher.*—The teacher will find that the observance of these directions will conduce much to the neatness of a composition. He is requested to explain them to the pupil, and is advised to insist on their being followed.

A relative is properly addressed by the name that indicates the relationship; as, "My dear Father," "My dear Aunt," "My dear Nephew". Or, a relative or friend may be addressed by the Christian name, if intimacy will allow it; as, "My dear Sarah," "My dear William".

Give the proper date and address of a letter to Mr. Henry Anderson.

$$\left\{ \begin{array}{l} \textit{100 Bleecker St., N. Y.} \\ \textit{December 15th, 1868.} \end{array} \right.$$

Henry Anderson, Esq.

Dear Sir,

Describe the clause of respect at the close of a letter.

There are various clauses of respect, appropriate to different letters, according to the relative positions of the writer and the person addressed. A few of the most common are subjoined; the pupil will at once see in what cases each is appropriate.

I remain, my dear Sir,

Your faithful friend and

obedient servant,

*George H. Valentine.**

---

* *Note to the Pupil.*—Observe the punctuation of these signa-

Very respectfully and truly yours,

H. S. Peters.

Believe me, dear mother, as ever,

Your affectionate daughter,

Ellen.

Rest assured that you have the best wishes of

Your sincere friend,

G. Seaman Gray.

EXERCISE.

Copy according to these directions, and punctuate the letter given below, which is supposed to have been written from the following heads, by a young man on a voyage :—

ANALYSIS.

I. Acknowledgment of the reception of letters from home.

tures. When the initial letter is used for a name, a period should be placed after it, to denote the abbreviation. A period should be placed after the surname also.

II. Feelings after starting.
III. Sea-sickness.
IV. Storm.
 V. Arrival at Rio Janeiro.

N. B. In letters of friendship, the first line of the address, containing the name and title, is generally omitted.

Rio Janeiro, July 9th, 1868.

My dear Father,

You who have been such a traveller must know the pleasure afforded one that is separated from his family by the receipt of letters from home you may therefore imagine my delight on beholding the full budget which awaited my arrival here I had hardly ventured to hope for letters lest I might be disappointed for though we had tarried some time at Trinidad I was fearful that no other vessel would have arrived at Rio Janeiro before us My apprehensions however were soon put to flight by the reception of a most welcome package from which I was glad to see that I had not been forgotten by any member of our little household

While preparations were being made for my leaving home I looked forward to my proposed voyage with ardent anticipations of pleasure But when the moment for starting arrived and I was called upon to bid farewell to all that were nearest and dearest my heart was full of sorrow and I bitterly regretted that it had been thought best for me to go When the pilot-boat left us and your form my dear father gradually faded from my view I could no longer restrain my feelings but burst into a flood of tears The recollection of the friends and beloved relatives that I had left behind me and of the possibility that I might never meet them again on earth overwhelmed me with sorrow

How long these feelings might have continued I do not know but on the second day out a fresh breeze sprung up the sea became quite rough and my mind was called away from its gloomy reflections by a sudden fit of sea-sickness Much as I had read in travellers' note-books respecting this most disagreeable companion of a sea-voyage I did not realize a tithe of its discomfort until I became a victim of it myself For three days I lay in my berth without tasting food in a state of perfect in-difference to all that was going on around and heartily sorry that I had ever consented

> " to roam
> O'er the dark sea-foam "

On the morning of our sixth day out I felt a little better and though my brain was so dizzy that I could hardly see and my limbs seemed almost unable to sup-port me I attempted to get up Not till then was I aware that we were in the midst of a terrible storm The vessel was plunging and the timbers were creaking as if every instant they must part while ever and anon above the howlings of the gale were heard the hoarse tones of the Captain shouting through his speaking-trumpet to the men Full of fear I managed to creep back into my berth and it was not until near evening I learned that for the past twenty-four hours we had experienced one of the heaviest gales ever known off Cape Hatteras

The remainder of our voyage was not marked by any incident worthy of narration We arrived here this morning and I hasten to despatch this letter to relieve your anxiety There are as you may suppose many interesting objects in this city these together with the

beautiful bay and the surrounding country I shall at,
tempt to describe in my next

Remember me affectionately to each member of our
family   I shall write to them all at the next opportunity   For yourself my dear father accept the best
wishes and grateful love of

Your affectionate son

JACOB PERRY, JR.

----◆----

LESSON LXV.

LETTER-WRITING.

WHAT is requisite in business letters ?

Business letters should be as short as possible,
and confined strictly to the subject in hand.

Give an example of the proper form of address to a Firm.

The following is an example of the proper form :

Messrs. Parker & Tillotson :—

Gentlemen,

How should a letter be folded ?

As envelopes are now generally used for enclosing letters, the most convenient way of folding is
as follows:—As the sheet lies before you, turn up
the bottom until its edge exactly lies upon the edge
at the top, and make a fold in the middle.   The
sheet is now in an oblong form.   Bring the side
that is at your right hand toward your body, and
fold over about one-third of the letter toward the
top ; finally, turn as much of the upper part over

in the opposite direction, and the sheet is properly folded for enclosing in an envelope.*

What is meant by the superscription of a letter?

The direction on the outside, consisting of the name of the person addressed, the name of the place, and the state in which he lives. Thus :—

Hector McNiel, Esq.

Grenada,

Mississippi.

In the superscription, what common error must be avoided?

The use of two titles that imply the same thing. Thus, instead of directing to "*Mr.* William Walton, *Esq.*," we should direct either to "*Mr.* William Walton," or to "William Walton, *Esq.*"

Correct the following direction: "*Dr.* James Purple, M. D."

EXERCISE.

Write a letter according to the analysis given below. Follow the directions for dating, addressing, folding, and superscribing; above all, let your letter contain no bad spelling or incorrect punctuation. The pupil will imagine that he is writing from a boarding-school, in Salem, Massachusetts, to a sister at home, in New York City.

---

* *Note.* — As a practical illustration seems necessary, the teacher is requested to fold a sheet of letter-paper for the pupil according to these directions.

ANALYSIS.

I. Acknowledge receipt of a letter from home, and state the feelings it awakened.

II. Describe the weather, and state its effect on the spirits and amusements of the scholars.

III. Give an account of the daily routine of exercises in the school.

IV. Describe the teacher.

V. State when the next holiday occurs; how it is anticipated by the scholars; how they will spend it; state your feelings with regard to your anticipated return home.

———

LESSON LXVI.

EXERCISE IN LETTER-WRITING.

WRITE a letter from Poughkeepsie, N. Y., to your grandmother at Danbury, Conn., according to the following analysis. Date, &c., as directed. Do not use the words of the analysis, where it can be avoided.

I. Express satisfaction at having heard, through your father, who has just returned from Danbury, that her health continues good; hope that you may see her before long, so as to judge for yourself.

II. Tell how Poughkeepsie is situated. Describe the Hudson River. Speak of the frequent communication with New York by means of the Hudson River Railroad, and the superior advantages thus afforded for travel and transportation, particularly when the river is frozen, &c.

III. Give an account of the way in which you spend Sunday; describe the place of worship which you attend. Describe your new clergyman. Tell what his text was last Sunday, and describe his sermon.

IV. Ask your grandmother to write to you often, and to state in her next letter when she will come to Poughkeepsie; state how glad you will be to see her, and what amusements you have devised to interest her.

——◆——

LESSON LXVII.

DESCRIPTION.

WHAT is the second division embraced under the head of prose composition?

Descriptions.

In what does Description consist?

Description consists in noting down the characteristics or peculiarities of any particular object.

To write a description, what is necessary?

For the writer to be familiar with what he is attempting to describe.

Do descriptions admit of analysis?

Yes; all subjects of composition do.

Before commencing your description, then, what will it be best to do?

To analyze the subject, according to the directions already given.*

* *Note to the Teacher.*—It will be well for the teacher to insist

What objects admit of description?

All objects that meet the eye.

What are the three classes of objects that writers are most frequently called on to describe?

I. Material objects; such as *houses, ships,* &c.

II. Natural scenery.

III. Persons.

In describing the first of these classes, material objects, what heads will generally be found appropriate?

All of the following heads may not be appropriate in each case, but a selection may be made of such as are :—

I. The place where the object was seen; the time when it was made, invented, or discovered; its history.

II. The purpose for which it was designed.

III. The materials of which, and the persons by whom, it was made.

IV. Its form, size, and general appearance.

V. Compare it with any other object which it may resemble.

VI. The effects it has produced.

VII. The feelings excited by beholding it.

EXERCISE.

Copy and punctuate the following description; observe its characteristics carefully. Use capital letters where they are required.

---

that an analysis be drawn up, in all cases, before the pupil proceeds to his composition. Besides imparting precision to the mind, this practice will insure a proper arrangement in the composition.

THE GREAT CLOCK OF STRASBURG.

There is no subject that i can think of which will be so likely to interest you as the great astronomical clock which i saw the other day in the cathedral at strasburg. this cathedral by the way is one of the finest and oldest in europe. it is twenty-four feet higher than the great pyramid in egypt and one hundred and forty feet higher than st pauls in london. the astronomical clock stands in the inside in one corner of it and is a most imposing and beautiful edifice. five or six hundred people visit it every day at twelve o'clock when it performs some extraordinary feats which I shall presently mention

There have been two or three clocks in the same place upon the model of which the present one is formed but it is almost a new one. it was constructed in 1838 by a mechanic named schwilque to whom a festival was given by his fellow-citizens on the occasion of its completion

To give you some idea of the size of this clock i will inform you that it is as high and about as wide as the old state-house in washington street boston there are means of going into the inside of it and ten or fifteen people perhaps more may stand in its very heart and examine the machinery mr neale two other gentlemen and myself with the conductor went into it and spent about an hour there we went first into a lower then into a higher and then into a still higher apartment of it and saw the various parts of the machinery they consisted i should think of more than a thousand pieces splendidly polished and all dependent for their harmonious action upon the short thick brass pendulum which swings in the centre

This clock points out not only the hours and the
7

days but the times and the seasons the revolutions of
the stars the solar and lunar equations the conjunctions
and eclipses of the heavenly bodies their positions at
any given time and the various changes through which
they pass for thousands of years it points out apparent
time mean or real time and ecclesiastical time on its
face you see the motions of the stars of the sun and
planets of the moon and her satellites two little cherubs
who sit the one on one side the other on the other
strike the *quarters* of the hour death strikes the *hour*
with a mace while four figures pass and repass before
him representing the various stages of human life

Every day when death strikes twelve the apostles
who are represented each with the sign of his martyr-
dom come out from the clock and pass before an image
of the saviour bowing as they pass and receiving his
benediction which he gives with a movement of the
head when the apostle peter makes his appearance a
gilded cock which is perched on one side of the clock
flaps his wings raises his head and crows so long and
so loud as to make the whole cathedral ring again this
he repeats three times in memorial of the cock that
crowed three times before the fall of Peter during the
crucifixion of our saviour of course the cock makes
no further noise or motion till the next day at twelve
o'clock when he repeats the same loud and startling
crow flapping his wings and raising his head

Now i dare say you will all exclaim what a wonderful clock what a wonderful man must he be that made
it but let us remember how much more wonderful are
the mechanism of the universe and the god who made
it how wonderful that being who made us and all mankind and keeps the whole universe going and every

heart beating from day to day and from year to year "Lo these are but a part of his ways but the thunder of his power who can understand"

———◆———

LESSON LXVIII.

DESCRIPTION.

WRITE a description of A SHIP according to the analysis given on page 133, omitting the third and fourth heads entirely, and enlarging on the second and sixth.

———◆———

LESSON LXIX.

DESCRIPTION OF NATURAL SCENERY.

IN describing natural scenery, what heads is it best to take? Selections may be made from the following :—

I. The circumstances under which it was seen; whether at sunrise, at noon, or by moonlight; the effect, &c.

II. The natural features of the scene; whether level or undulating; whether fertile or barren, &c.

III. The improvements made by man; whether well cultivated; whether any buildings are in sight; if so, describe them.

IV. The figures in the scene; if any human beings, describe them.

V. The neighboring inhabitants; their character, peculiarities, &c.

VI. The sounds that meet the ear; as, the murmur of a stream, the noise of a waterfall, the rustling of the leaves under the influence of the wind, the lowing of cattle, the barking of dogs, the singing of birds, the cries of children; the sounds of industry, such as the noise of machinery, &c.

VII. The distant prospect.

VIII. A comparison with any other scene which it may resemble.

IX. The historical associations connected with the scene.

X. The feelings which the view awakened in the mind.

Is it necessary for these heads to be considered in the order given above?

No; they may be taken in any order that may suit the convenience of the writer.

EXERCISE.

Copy and punctuate the following description written by Sir Walter Scott. Observe its characteristics. Use capitals where they are required.

AN ANCIENT YORKSHIRE FOREST SCENE.

" in that pleasant district of merry england which is watered by the river don there extended in ancient times a large forest covering the greater part of the beautiful hills and valleys which lie between sheffield and the pleasant town of doncaster. the remains of this extensive wood are still to be seen at the noble seats of wentworth of wharncliffe park and around rotherham. here haunted of yore the fabulous dragon of wantley here were fought many of the most desperate battles during the civil wars of the roses and here also flourished in ancient times those bands of gallant outlaws whose deeds have been rendered so popular in english song. * * * *

the sun was setting upon one of the rich grassy glades of the forest that has been mentioned. hundreds of broad-headed short-stemmed wide-branched oaks which had witnessed perhaps the stately march of the roman soldiery flung their gnarled arms over a thick carpet of the most delicious greensward in some places they were intermingled with beeches hollies and copsewood of various descriptions so closely as totally to intercept the level beams of the sinking sun in others they receded from each other forming those long sweeping vistas in the intricacy of which the eye delights to lose itself while imagination considers them as the paths to yet wilder scenes of sylvan solitude. here the red rays of the sun shot a broken and discolored light that partially hung upon the shattered boughs and mossy trunks of the trees and there they illuminated in brilliant patches the portions of turf to which they made their way. a considerable open space in the midst of this glade seemed formerly to have been dedicated to the rites of druidical superstition for on the summit of a hillock so regular as to seem artificial there still remained part of a circle of rough unhewn stones of large dimensions. seven stood upright the rest had been dislodged from their places probably by the zeal of some convert to christianity and lay some prostrate near their former site and others on the side of the hill. one large stone only had found its way to the bottom and in stopping the course of a small brook which glided smoothly round the foot of the eminence gave by its opposition a feeble voice of murmur to the placid and elsewhere silent streamlet.

the human figures which completed this landscape were in number two partaking in their dress and appearance of that wild and rustic character which belonged to the woodlands of the west riding of yorkshire at that early period."

(Here follows a description of the persons.)

LESSON LXX.

EXERCISE IN DESCRIPTION.

WRITE a description of the "Scene from Fort Lee Bluff," according to the hints in the following analysis. Do not use the words of the book, but express the thoughts in your own language.

I. Alone; sunrise; appearance of the sun as it gradually emerges above the eastern horizon.

II. Eye rests first on the Hudson flowing at the base of the bluff; effect of water on a landscape. On the opposite side, a fine country, hill and valley, studded with villages.

III. While in the distance many evidences of cultivation meet the eye of one looking eastward, on the west is an unbroken forest, not even an occasional house; one might suppose that he were in a wilderness far from civilization, were it not for one evidence of human industry and ingenuity, a high post for the telegraph wire, which here crosses the river. Remarks on this great enterprise.

IV. No person in view; sloops with white sails look like large birds.

V. While the eye is thus pleased, the ear is no less delighted; describe some of the sounds that usually meet the ear in the country on a summer morning.

VI. Feelings awakened; contrast with the excitement of a city life; the grandeur and beauty of the scene lead the mind to the Creator, and a thanksgiving goes up to him from the heart— (for what?)

LESSON LXXI.

DESCRIPTION OF PERSONS.

In what varieties of composition is the writer most frequently called on to describe persons?

In biographical sketches, travels, history, and novels.

In describing persons, what heads is it best to take?

A selection may be made from the following :—

I. Person; whether tall or short, fleshy or thin.

II. Dress.

III. Face; features; expression.

IV. Manners; whether dignified, graceful, awkward, active, indolent, haughty, or affable.

V. Any peculiarity of appearance.

EXERCISE.

Copy and punctuate the following description of "Leather-stocking," extracted from one of Cooper's novels :—

LEATHER-STOCKING.

" There was a peculiarity in the manner of the hunter
that struck the notice of the young female who had been
a close and interested observer of his appearance and
equipments from the moment he first came into view
He was tall and so meagre as to make him seem above
even the six feet that he actually stood in his stockings
On his head which was thinly covered with lank sandy
hair he wore a cap made of fox-skin His face was skinny
and thin almost to emaciation but yet bore no signs of
disease on the contrary it had every indication of the
most robust and enduring health The cold and the ex-
posure had together given it a color of uniform red his
gray eyes were glancing under a pair of shaggy brows
that overhung them in long hairs of gray mingled with
their natural hue his scraggy neck was bare and burnt
to the same tint with his face though a small part of a
shirt-collar made of the country check was to be seen
above the over-dress he wore   A kind of coat made of
dressed deer-skin with the hair on was belted close to his
lank body by a girdle of colored worsted   On his feet
were deer-skin moccasins ornamented with porcupines'
quills after the manner of the Indians and his limbs
were guarded with long leggings of the same material as
the moccasins which gartering over the knees of his tar-
nished buck-skin breeches had obtained for him among
the settlers the nick-name of Leather-stocking notwithstanding his legs were protected beneath in winter by
thick garments of woollen duly made of good blue yarn
Over his left shoulder was slung a belt of deer-skin from
which depended an enormous ox-horn so thinly scraped
as to discover the dark powder that it contained   The

larger end was fitted ingeniously and securely with a wooden bottom and the other was stopped tight by a little plug A leathern pouch hung before him from which as he concluded his last speech he took a small measure and filling it accurately with powder he commenced reloading the rifle which as its butt rested on the snow before him reached nearly to the top of his fox-skin cap "

LESSON LXXII.

EXERCISES IN DESCRIPTION.

WRITE descriptions of

A RAILROAD.

THE COUNTRY IN SUMMER.

[N. B. The pupil is expected *in every case* to prepare an analysis of his subject, before he proceeds to the composition itself. This will not, therefore, be repeated in the directions. If he meets with difficulty in drawing out his analyses, it will be well for him to review Lesson LXIII., which treats of that subject.]

LESSON LXXIII.

NARRATION.

WHAT is the third division embraced under the head of prose composition ?

Narrations.

In what does Narration consist ?

In giving a detailed account of incidents which

have taken place, or which the writer imagines to
have taken place.

When the incidents have no foundation in fact, but are created
by the imagination of the writer, what is the composition called?

Fiction.

What are the principal divisions embraced under the general
head of fiction?

Tales, Novels, and Romances.

When confined to fact, what are the principal divisions embraced under the head of narration?

I. History; or, an account of general incidents.

II. Biography; or, an account of incidents in
the lives of individuals.

III. Travels and Voyages; or, accounts of incidents that have happened to persons while
away from home, or while traversing the
ocean.

In narration, must we confine ourselves strictly to an account
of the incidents?

No; we may with advantage introduce descriptions of scenes, and of the persons concerned.

In narration, what is particularly necessary?

That the sentences be clear, and the connection
between the parts be properly maintained.

EXERCISE.

Copy and punctuate the following specimen of
historical narration, which is based on the Scrip-
tural account of Belshazzar's Feast in the 5th
chapter of the book of Daniel. The pupil is requested to turn to this chapter; he will find that

the language used in the extract below is *entirely different* from that of the Bible. From this he will understand what is meant, when, in following an outline given in the book, he is directed *to use his own language.*

BELSHAZZAR'S FEAST

" It was night but the usual stillness of that hour was broken by the sounds of feasting and revelry It had been a festival day in Babylon and the inhabitants had not yet sunk into repose The song and the dance still continued and the voice of music was heard All seemed in perfect security and no precautions had been taken to avoid the danger which hung over their devoted heads An invading army was even then surrounding the walls of the city but those who ought to have defended it confident and secure left it unguarded and exposed to the attacks of the enemy Fear was excluded even from the walls of the palace and the monarch was giving his own example of rioting and mirth to his subjects A thousand of the noblest lords in his kingdom were feasting with him as his invited guests They had ' already tarried long at the wine ' when Belshazzar in the pride and impiety of his heart commanded the servants to bring the silver and golden vessels which had been taken by his grandfather Nebuchadnezzar from the temple at Jerusalem They were brought and filled with wine and as they drank it they extolled their gods of wood and of stone

But while they were thus sacrilegiously employed their mirth was suddenly changed into amazement and consternation A hand like that of a man was seen to write upon the wall of the palace and as they gazed upon it it traced the sentence 'Mene, Mene, Tekel, Upharsin' No one among the vast company understood its meaning but to their affrighted imagination it was full of portentous import The king who was exceedingly terrified sent in haste for all the astrologers and those persons in whose powers of divination he had been accustomed to place confidence but none could explain the mysterious warning

At this juncture the queen entered and informed the king that Daniel was in the city and that he was supposed to possess the wisdom of the gods He was hastily summoned into the royal presence and after reproving the trembling monarch for the pride which he had manifested revealed to him the doom which was pronounced upon him He told him that his kingdom and his own life were nearly at a close that his empire should be divided between the Medes and Persians and also that his own character had been examined and found lamentably deficient

The reward which had been promised was now bestowed upon Daniel He was arrayed in a kingly robe adorned with a golden chain and proclaimed the third in authority in the kingdom Ere the next rising sun Belshazzar was numbered with the dead"

LESSON LXXIV.

EXERCISE IN HISTORICAL NARRATION.

WRITE *in your own language* an account of "The Casting of Daniel into the Den of Lions," from the facts recorded in the 6th chapter of the book of Daniel. Attach to it such reflections on the preservation of Daniel, and the destruction of his wicked enemies, as suggest themselves to your mind.

LESSON LXXV.

EXERCISE IN HISTORICAL NARRATION.

WRITE *in your own language* an extended account of the incidents described in the following outlines. In doing this you may have occasion to follow the directions given in Lessons XLIII., XLIV., XLV., XLVI., and LII.

ROMAN VIRTUE.

Pyrrhus was king of Epirus. The Samnites were at war with Rome; they invited Pyrrhus to help them. He accepted their invitation. The physician of Pyrrhus was a bad man; he told the Romans that, for a large reward, he would poison his master. Fabricius was the Roman general; he was an honorable man; he was shocked at the physician's treachery, and sent the traitor away with scorn, saying, "We should be honorable even to our enemies." Pyrrhus heard of this; he would not be outdone in generosity; he sent his prisoners to Rome without ransom, and consented to negotiate a peace.

[Close with reflections on the baseness of such treachery, and the policy of always pursuing an honorable course, as the Romans did on this occasion.]

THE DISOBEDIENT CAPTAIN.

Frederick II., the Great, king of Prussia, was a famous warrior; remarkable for strict discipline. In one of his campaigns he intended, during the night, to make an important movement; gave orders that every light in the camp should be put out at eight o'clock, on pain of death. At that hour he went out himself, to see if the order was obeyed. Saw one light; in the tent of Captain Zietern; king entered; Zietern was folding a letter. Zietern was dismayed at beholding the king; threw himself on his knees and implored pardon; said he was writing to his wife, and had retained the candle to finish his letter. The king told him to go on, and write one line more which he would dictate to him; that line was to inform his wife that by sunrise the next day he would be a dead man. The letter was sent; at the appointed time Zietern was executed.

[Close with reflections on the necessity and policy of obedience.]

LESSON LXXVI.

BIOGRAPHICAL SKETCHES.

WHAT is a Biographical Sketch ?

A Biographical Sketch is a narration of the principal events in the life of an individual.

What is it proper to include in a biographical sketch ?

A description of the person under consideration, according to the heads given in Lesson LXXI.

What other particulars are to be considered in a biographical sketch ?

I. Birth, condition in life, vocation.

II. Character, disposition.

III. Mental abilities, leading characteristics of mind.

IV. Successive events, beginning at the earliest period of life.

V. His peculiarities, or what rendered him famous.

How do biographical sketches rank among other pieces of composition?

They are among the most interesting and useful.

What renders them useful?

They are useful, because the lives of the most distinguished men teach us that a course of uprightness and industry secures the respect of the world, and that idleness and vice bring their votaries to suffering and disgrace.

What length is proper for biographical sketches?

They may be of any length. Some men's lives are so eventful as to furnish sufficient matter for volumes. When brevity is required, only a few of the leading facts may be presented, and the whole may be so abridged as to occupy but a few pages, or even a single page.

EXERCISE.

Copy and punctuate the following specimen of a biographical sketch :—

MAHOMET.

"Mahomet was born at Mecca in 569 A D The tribe from which he descended was that of the Korash-

ites and the most noble in Arabia   His immediate an-
cestors seem however to have been undistinguished and
though his natural talents were great it is certain that
his education was inconsiderable   He acquired knowledge but not from books   Intercourse with mankind
had sharpened his faculties and given him an insight
into the human heart

In 609 when he was about 40 years old he began to
concert a system of measures the issue of which was the
establishment of a new religion in the world and of an
empire which spreading over many countries lasted
more than six centuries   The religion still remains

His impostures were not at first well received   The
citizens of Mecca even opposed them   Forsaking his native city where his life was in jeopardy he fled to Medina
at the epoch called by the Mahometans the hegira or
flight which was in the year 622   By the aid of his dis-
ciples at Medina he returned to Mecca as a conqueror
and making numerous proselytes he soon became master
of Arabia and Syria and was saluted as king in 627

The main arguments which Mahomet employed to
persuade men to embrace his religion were promises and
threats which he knew would easily work on the minds
of the multitude   His promises related chiefly to Paradise and to the sensual delights to be enjoyed in that
region of pure waters shady groves and exquisite fruits
Such a heaven had strong charms for the Arabians whose
burning climate made them regard images of this sort
with excessive pleasure   His threats on the other hand
were peculiarly terrific to this people   Those who rejected his religion were in the next world to drink nothing
but putrid and boiling water to breathe nothing but exceedingly hot winds they were to dwell for ever in con-

tinual fire intensely burning and be surrounded with a black hot salt smoke as with a coverlet

Mahomet was distinguished for the beauty of his person he had a commanding presence a majestic aspect piercing eyes a flowing beard and his whole countenance depicted the strong emotions of his mind His memory was retentive his wit easy and his judgment clear and decisive In his intercourse with society he observed the forms of that grave and ceremonious politeness so common in his country

Mahomet persisted in his fanaticism to the last On his death-bed he asserted that the angel of death was not allowed to take his soul till he had respectfully asked the permission of the prophet The request being granted Mahomet fell into the agony of dissolution he fainted with the violence of pain but recovering his spirits in a degree he raised his eyes upward and looking steadfastly said with a faltering voice O God pardon my sins Yes I come among my fellow-citizens on high and in this manner expired "

LESSON LXXVII.

EXERCISE IN BIOGRAPHICAL NARRATION.

WRITE, *in your own language*, a biographical sketch of Newton, from the facts furnished below. You may adopt whatever arrangement is most convenient.

SIR ISAAC NEWTON.

The most illustrious philosopher and mathematician that ever lived. Born, 1642, at Woolsthorpe, Lincolnshire, England. Lost his father when very young; his mother took great care of his early education. At 18, entered Trinity College, Cambridge; here he devoted himself to mathematics; displayed great ability in the various branches of that science. At 22, discovered the method of fluxions, which, however, he afterward greatly simplified and improved. Next, made important improvements in telescopes, by the grinding of optical glasses. Next, began to investigate the prism, and put forth a new theory respecting light and colors. His next discovery startled the whole world—this was the principle of gravitation. He was led to this by seeing an apple fall, while he was reclining under a tree in an orchard; his inquiring mind at once set about investigating the cause. His great work entitled "Principia" was published in 1687; this added much to his reputation, and procured him the respect of the learned and scientific of all countries. The friendship of Lord Halifax obtained for him the lucrative situation of master of the mint.

At 80, he became affected with a painful disease, which, five years later, proved fatal. Suffered great agony during the last five weeks of his life; bore it patiently; even smiled, while the paroxysms caused large drops of sweat to roll down his cheeks.

Newton was amiable; a Christian; studied the Bible much. Always rebuked irreverence. He was of middling height; his countenance, venerable and pleasant. His power of mind is universally admitted. A great writer has said that, if the learned men of all ages could meet in one assembly, they would choose Sir Isaac Newton for their president.

LESSON LXXVIII.

FICTION.

WHAT is Fiction?

Fiction is a species of composition in which events are narrated that have no foundation except in the imagination of the writer.

What make fiction interesting?

Striking scenes and novel combinations of events.

Repeat the three divisions that are embraced under the head of fiction.

Tales, novels, and romances.

What is the difference between a tale and a novel?

A novel is longer than a tale.

What is the difference between a novel and a romance?

A novel is founded on events that resemble those of real life; while a romance is a narration of wilder and more unnatural incidents.

In fiction, what other species of composition may be introduced with advantage?

Description and historical narration.

EXERCISE

An extract illustrative of fiction is unnecessary, as the pupil will recognize specimens of it in the various stories and fairy-tales which he has read.

Imagine that you had an encounter with banditti, while travelling in Italy, and write an account of it according to the following hints:—

THE BANDIT OF THE APENNINES.

Describe the scene; pass in the Apennines; night;

moon struggling with clouds. I was travelling in a large comfortable carriage; cold; sleepy.

Suddenly carriage stopped. Voices; oaths; traces cut; door opened; ferocious fellow masked; presented pistol; demanded money. Felt for pistols; not in their place; must have been removed by postilion; in league with the banditti. Had to give up money and jewels.

One ring had been given me by my mother; prized it much; asked the leader to let me retain it; he handed it to me with a polite bow, so much like the courteous salutation of the inn-keeper at the last stopping-place, that I could not help fancying that they were one and the same man.

Stripped me of all they could get; tied me to a tree; shouted; did no good. Was obliged to stay there till morning; a Count passed by with a large retinue of servants. Released me.

Six months after this was in Florence. There was to be a public execution. I happened to be out, and met the procession that was conducting the criminal to the gallows. They told me that he was one of the most daring bandits of the Apennines. Our eyes met; with imperturbable politeness he rose in the car, all manacled as he was, and made me that same bow to which I could have sworn among a thousand. It was no other than my host of the mountain-inn, and my polite friend of the mountain-pass. It was his last bow; in less than an hour his body was dangling from the gallows.

LESSON LXXIX.

ESSAYS.

WHAT is the third division embraced under the head of prose composition?

Essays.

What is an Essay?

An Essay is a composition, generally on some abstract subject, devoted rather to an investigation of causes, effects, &c., than to an examination of visible and material peculiarities.

May essays ever contain description or narration?

Yes; brief descriptions and narrations may be introduced into essays with advantage.

In essays, what heads is it proper to take?

Almost any that occur to the mind.

What name has been given to essays that treat of the principles of art, science, or moral truth?

Philosophical Essays.

EXERCISE.

WRITE an essay on COMMERCE according to the analysis given on page 132. It will be seen that the second, third, and fourth heads will introduce some historical narration; but this is not objectionable.

LESSON LXXX.

WRITE an essay on FRIENDSHIP, according to the following analysis:—

FRIENDSHIP.

I. DEFINITION. (What is friendship?)

II. ORIGIN. (Friendship took its rise in the social feelings implanted in the breast of man.)

III. ANTIQUITY. (Existed in the earliest times; much regarded by the ancients; Cicero composed a volume on it.)

IV. INSTANCES. (David and Jonathan; Damon and Pythias; &c. You may briefly relate the story of Damon and Pythias, if you are familiar with it.)

V. NECESSITY. (What would be the state of society without friendship?)

VI. EFFECTS.

——◆——

LESSON LXXXI.

ARGUMENTATIVE DISCOURSES.

WHAT is the fifth division embraced under the head of prose composition?

Argumentative Discourses.

What is an Argumentative Discourse?

An Argumentative Discourse is a composition in which the writer lays down a proposition, and attempts to persuade others that it is true.

What are the facts and reasons which a writer brings forward to sustain his position, called?

Arguments.

What are argumentative discourses called, when delivered before popular assemblies?

When on sacred subjects, they are called Ser-

mons; when on other subjects, Speeches or Orations.

In the orations and argumentative discourses of the ancients,
what formal divisions were adopted?

Six regular divisions were adopted, viz. :—

I. The Exordium, or Introduction; in which
the speaker strove to make his hearers attentive, and disposed to receive his arguments.

II. The Division, in which the speaker stated
the plan he intended to pursue in treating
the subject.

III. The Statement, in which the subject and
the facts connected with it, were laid open.

IV. The Reasoning, in which the arguments
were set forth in order, the weakest being
generally in the middle, and in which the
reasoning of opponents was refuted.

V. The Appeal to the Feelings, one of the most
important divisions of the discourse.

VI. The Peroration, in which the speaker sum-
med up all that had been said, and brought
his discourse to a close.

Is it customary to adopt this arrangement and division in discourses at the present day?

It is with some speakers; but others use less
formal divisions. There are many excellent discourses, in which several of these parts are altogether wanting.

EXERCISE.

Copy and punctuate the following specimen of

a short argumentative discourse.   It will be seen
that the regular division is not strictly adhered to.

HAPPINESS IS NOT ALWAYS THE REWARD OF VIRTUE

In contemplating the maxims of the ancient Stoic
philosophers we can not help being struck with the
soundness of their principles and the stern requirements
of their moral code   Yet there is one of their propositions to which we can not yield assent and that is that
temporal happiness is the necessary consequence of
virtue   So important a question one on which so many
issues and those the practical issues of life are staked
is well worthy of discussion

In treating the question it is well understood that
prejudices will have to be combated and removed for
there are many who without having looked closely at
the subject have followed the ancient Stoics and because it is a convenient creed to teach and one which it is
believed will lead to the practice of virtue have sought
to inculcate this selfish principle   A regard for virtue
should be instilled by higher arguments than this virtue should be practised because it is a duty because it
is the command of God

In the first place I lay down the proposition that
there is no necessary connection between virtue and
happiness   To the ancients who knew not that the
soul was immortal it may have seemed necessary that
the patient self-denial the forgiving charity and the active benevolence of virtue should be rewarded in this
world but we who live in the light of a revelation from
on high know that there is a hereafter and look to that
infinite cycle of ages not to this finite state of probation
for that degree of reward which virtue may procure

But again no one can deny that it is an important principle of our religious system that the virtuous and the pious should be put to the trial and that afflictions and crosses are sent by the Omnipotent to test the stability of their faith and practice As Job a man that "feared God and eschewed evil" was tried by visitations from on high so have the good of all ages been obliged to submit to similar probation Viewed in this light it would seem that trial is peculiarly in this world the lot of virtue the necessary preparation to be made in time by those who would enjoy a blissful eternity

But those who with the poet believe that

"Virtue alone is happiness below"

point us to the pleasures of a quiet conscience and the peace which a knowledge of the performance of duty brings with it It is admitted that these are great blessings and that without them happiness can not exist but are they alone sufficient to make a man happy Can the quietest conscience in the universe remove the pangs of hunger alleviate the sufferings of the sick or comfort the mourner The experience of the world will answer no There are many Jobs there are many good but unhappy men

To go a step further to say what is necessary to insure happiness to point to religion the hope of that which is to come as an anchor to which the soul may cling "amid a sea of trouble" would be foreign to the question In view of the arguments we have advanced in view of the striking argument furnished by our own experience we think we may fairly conclude that

"Virtue alone is" *not* "happiness below"
8

LESSON LXXXII.

FIGURES.—SIMILE.

[The pupil is now familiar with the principal kinds of composition. All that remains to complete the course, is a few lessons on the principal figures.]

WHEN we say, " *Saladin was a fox in the council, a lion in the field*," do we mean that he actually became at one time a fox, and at another a lion?

No; we mean that he was cunning in laying plans, and bold in executing them.

When language is used in this way to represent, not the idea which the words really express, but some thought that is analogous or has some resemblance to them, how is it said to be used?

Figuratively.

What are the principal figures?

Simile, Metaphor, and Personification.

What is Simile?

Simile is a figure by which we liken one thing to another.

Give an example.

" *Good nature,* like the sun, *sheds a light on all around.*"

In making similes, what must we observe?

That the objects compared have a resemblance.

What words are used to introduce similes?

Like and *as.*

For what two purposes are similes used?

Similes are used,

 I. For illustrating or explaining the meaning; such similes are called *explaining* similes.

 II. For embellishing the style; they are then called *embellishing* similes.

What rules are to be observed in using similes?

I. Objects that are little known should be compared to things that are better known.

II. Objects should be likened to other objects
which possess the quality in which they
resemble each other in a higher degree
than themselves. Thus, in the sentence,
" *The moon is like a jewel in the sky,*"
the simile is bad, because the *moon* sheds
more light than a *jewel*, and should not
be compared to it.

EXERCISE.

Complete the following sentences by introducing
a simile wherever a dash occurs. Remember that
similes are introduced by the words *like* and *as*.

EXAMPLE. Temptations, ——, beset him on every
side.

Completed. Temptations, *like so many snares*, beset him on every side.

1. He who is a traitor to his country is —— which
turns to bite the bosom that warms it.

2. Richelieu upheld the state —— which supports
the weight of a whole edifice.

3. Anger —— consumes the heart.

4. Her eyes —— shed a mild radiance on all around.

5.　　　Her brow was —— fair,
　　　　Her cheeks —— red.

6. Satan goes about ——, seeking whom he may
devour.

7. A virtuous man slandered by his enemies, is
like ——.

8. She was as unsuspicious —— which "licks the hand just raised to shed its blood."

9. She mourns —— which has lost its mate.

10. Sorrow shades the soul, as a cloud ——.

11. He is as firm —— which rears its head unmoved above the billows.

12. Man is —— which to-day springeth up and bloometh, and to-morrow withereth away.

13. Shakspeare tells us that Desdemona's skin was as white as ——, and as smooth ——.

14. He stood silent and motionless ——.

—•—

LESSON LXXXIII.

METAPHOR.

WHAT is the most common figure?

Metaphor.

What is Metaphor?

Metaphor is a comparison in which the words denoting the similitude are omitted; as, " *Good nature is a sun which sheds light on all around.*"

How may a simile be converted into a metaphor?

By omitting the word *like* or *as*, and slightly altering the construction of the sentence, as may be required by this omission.

Give an example.

" *Vice*, like *a Siren, sings her songs in the ears of youth ;* " here we have a simile. By omitting *like*, and slightly altering the sentence, we convert the simile into a metaphor ; thus, " *Vice is a Siren that sings her songs in the ears of youth.*"

What is essential to the effect of a metaphor?

That the resemblance between the objects compared should be evident.

Is it well to crowd a number of metaphors together into a
small compass?

It is not; they lose their effect, when used in
too great abundance.

What is the most important rule relating to the use of metaphors?

Always carry out the figure; that is, after having introduced a metaphor, do not in the same sentence return to the use of plain language.

Give an example in which this rule is violated.

Pope, in his translation of Homer's Odyssey,
makes Penelope, when speaking of her son, say,

> "Now from my fond embrace by tempests torn,
> Our other column of the state is borne,
> Nor took a kind adieu, nor sought consent."

In the second line she calls her son a "*column of
the state*," and in the third speaks of his *taking a
kind adieu*, and *seeking consent*. Now, as *columns*
are not in the habit of *taking kind adieus* or *seeking consent*, there is an inconsistency, and the metaphor is faulty. The poet should either not have likened him to a column, or else should have assigned
to him no action that a column can not perform.

How may such metaphors be corrected?

By assigning to the leading object an action not
incompatible with the object to which it is compared.

Give an example.

"*A torrent of superstition consumed the land;*"

here the metaphor is faulty because *torrents* do not *consume.* We correct it by assigning to the leading object an action not incompatible with the nature of torrents; thus, "*A torrent of superstition* flowed over *the land.*"

What other rule must be observed with regard to metaphors?

They must be appropriate.

Give an example of an inappropriate metaphor.

The clergyman who prayed that 'God would be *a rock* to them that are afar off upon the sea,' used a very inappropriate metaphor, because, as *rocks* in the sea are a source of great danger to mariners, he was in reality asking for the destruction of those for whose safety he intended to pray.

EXERCISE.

1. Complete and alter sentences 1, 2, 3, 4, 6, and 7, in the Exercise at the close of the last Lesson, so that they may contain metaphors instead of similes. Remember that, in a metaphor, the comparison is not introduced by the word *like* or *as.*

2. Complete the following sentences so that they may contain metaphors:—

EXAMPLE.   The cares of riches are   with which we bind ourselves to earth.

Completed.   The cares of riches are *golden chains* with which we bind ourselves to earth.

1. Truth is a beautiful but simple ——, in which we should all seek to array ourselves.

2. Money is the —— which the miser worships.

3. He became involved in the —— of vice.

4. Honesty is a brighter —— than that which adorns a king's head.

5. Roman eloquence was —— of late growth.

6. When industry sows the ⎯ , the harvest is abundant.

7. Death is but a long ——, from which all shall one day awaken.

8. He is travelling the —— of pleasure.

9. The kindness of our Creator is —— from which all our blessings flow.

10. Love is a —— to which opposition only adds fuel.

LESSON LXXXIV.

EXERCISE IN METAPHORICAL LANGUAGE.

CONVERT the following *figurative* language into *plain* language which will express the same idea :—

EXAMPLE. The *evening of life.*

A *hard* heart.

In plain language. Old age.

An uncompassionate heart.

1. The *morning of life.* The *veil* of night. A *fiery* temper. A *deep* thinker. A *light* disposition. A *cold* heart. A *warm* friend.

2. We met with a *freezing* reception.

3. Richard was now *at the zenith* of his glory.

4. The earth *is thirsty.*

5. The sea *swallows* many a noble vessel.

6. Ajax was the *bulwark* of the Greeks.

7. His *hard* heart was *melted* by the speaker's *fire.*

Convert the following plain language into figurative language that will express the same idea. The words in parentheses after each sentence are intended to suggest an appropriate figure.

EXAMPLE. The meadows are covered with grass. (Clothed, robes.)

In figurative language. The meadows are clothed in their robes of green.

8. The ocean was calm. (Waves, asleep, bosom.)

9. In youth all things seem pleasant. (Morning, colored, roseate hue.)

10. A true friend will tell us of our faults. (Friend- ship, mirror.)

11. Let us renounce the dominion of the tyrant. (Cast off, yoke.)

12. Guilt is generally miserable. (Wedded.)

13. Hope is a great support in misfortune. (Anchor, soul clings, sea.)

14. Homer's poetry is more sublime than Virgil's. (Genius, soars higher.)

LESSON LXXXV.

PERSONIFICATION.

WHAT is Personification?

Personification is a figure by which we attribute life, sex, or action, to inanimate objects. Thus, when we say " the land *smiles* with plenty," we represent the earth as a living creature, *smiling*.

What effect has the judicious use of this figure upon style?

It enlivens and embellishes it, by bringing striking pictures before the mind.

What is meant by attributing sex to an inanimate object?

Speaking of it as *he* or *she;* thus we say of the sun, "He *sheds* his *light over hill and dale;*" of a ship, "*How bravely* she *rides the waves!*"

EXERCISE.

Make sentences, each of which shall contain one of the following words personified:—

EXAMPLE. War.

Sentence. War flings his blood-stained banner to the breeze.

Peace,	Religion,	A ship,	Spring,
Health,	Prosperity,	The wind,	Wisdom,
Time,	Industry,	The moon,	Vice,
Fire,	Pleasure,	The waves,	Night,
Summer,	Liberty,	The grave,	Death.

A LIST OF SUBJECTS.

THE pupil is now prepared for exercises in any department of prose composition. As a great deal of time is often lost in the selection of themes, a list of subjects is here subjoined, each of which, if properly treated, will be found sufficient for one exercise. They have been so arranged, as far as possible, as to make the progress in difficulty regular, but exceedingly gradual; and the author would advise that they be taken in turn, in the order in which they are here presented. It will be well for the teacher to prescribe some limit of length—that no composition, for instance, contain less than thirty lines of manuscript.

Before entering on this list of subjects, if there be any part of the book with which the pupil is not familiar, it will be best for him to review it.

LETTERS.

1. Write a letter to your teacher, giving an account of the manner in which you spent your last vacation.

2. Write to a friend, describing your sister's wedding, and the festivities on that occasion.

3. Write to a cousin in the country, giving an account of a concert, the Museum, or any place of public amusement which you may have recently visited.

4. Write to a parent, or other relative, travelling in Europe, about domestic matters.

5. Write an answer to the preceding letter, in which the parent would naturally give some account of his travels in Europe.

6. Announce in a letter to a friend that his brother whom you knew, and who resided in the same place that you do, is dead. Give an account of his sickness. Offer such consolation as is in your power.

7. Write a note to a friend, requesting the loan of a volume.

Write a note, inviting a friend to spend the holidays at your father's house.

Write a note, regretting that prior engagements will compel you to decline a friend's invitation.

8. Write a letter to a merchant, applying for a situation as clerk, and stating your qualifications.

Write an answer from the merchant.

DESCRIPTIONS.

9. An Elephant.
10. A Market.
11. A Farm.
12. A Canal.
13. A Hotel.
14. A Garden.
15. A Manufactory.
16. A Church.
17. A Fire-engine
18. A Dry-goods Store.
19. Describe "A Steamboat" and "A Ship"; tell wherein they differ, and wherein they are alike.
20. Treat in like manner "A Clock and a Watch".
21. A Bird and a Beast.
22. A Man and a Monkey.

23. A Snake and an Eel.
24. A Horse and a Cow.
25. A Sleigh and a Carriage.
26. Describe the place in which you live.
27. A Thunder-storm.
28. A Lake Scene.
29. A Storm at Sea.
30. The Country in Spring.
31. Scenes of Peace.
32. Scenes of War.
33. Contrast between a Morning and an Evening Scene.
34. A Scene in an Auction Room.
35. The Good Scholar.
36. The Idle Boy.
37. The Intemperate Man.
38. An Indian.
39. Thanksgiving Day.

NARRATIONS.

*Fiction.**

40. Adventures in California.
41. An Encounter with Pirates.
42. A Lion Hunt in Southern Africa.
43. The Indian's Revenge.
44. The History of a Pin.
45. The History of a Bible.
46. The History of a Cent.
47. The History of a Shoe.
48. The Story of an old Soldier.
49. Robinson Crusoe.

Historical Narrations.†

50. The Discovery of America.
51. The American Revolution.
52. The Reign of the Emperor Nero.
53. The Invasion of Russia by Napoleon.
54. The Crusades.
55. The Reformation.
56. The Crossing of the Red Sea. (Exodus, chap. xiv.)
57. David and Goliath. (I. Samuel, chap. xvii.)
58. Jephthah's Daughter. (Judges, chap. xi., verse 29.)
59. Naaman, the Leper. (II. Kings, chap. v.)
60. The History of Jonah.

---

* For the Exercises in Fiction it will be necessary to draw on the imagination; in some cases, it may be well for the teacher to assist the pupil with remarks on the subject. In the case of "the History of a Pin", it is necessary only to imagine some of the scenes that a pin would be likely to pass through, and to relate them as if the pin itself were speaking; thus, "The first recollections that *I* have," &c.

† In the Historical Narrations and Biographical Sketches, the pupil must obtain his facts from some history. He must clothe them, however, in his own language.

Biographical Sketches.

61. Washington.
62. Franklin.
63. Charlemagne.
64. Alfred the Great.
65. Shakspeare.
66. Queen Elizabeth.
67. Columbus.
68. Julius Cæsar.
69. Alexander the Great.
70. Homer.
71. Moses.
72. Ruth.
73. Solomon.
74. Daniel.

ESSAYS.

75. Spring.
76. The Beauties of Nature.
77. The Mariners' Compass.
78. The Advantages of Education.
79. Evening.
80. The Fickleness of Fortune.
81. Disease.
82. Chivalry.
83. Honesty.
84. The Ruins of Time.
85. Gambling.
86. The Study of History.
87. Youth.
88. Winter.
89. The Starry Heavens.
90. Government.
91. Old Age.
92. Anger.
93. Ambition.
94. Contentment.
95. The Sun.
96. City Life.
97. Life in the Country.
98. The Life of the Merchant.
99. The Life of the Sailor.
100. The Life of the Soldier.
101. Manufactures.
102. The Spirit of Discovery.
103. Newspapers.
104. Freedom.
105. The Art of Printing.
106. The Influence of Woman.
107. The Ocean.
108. The Pleasures of Travelling.
109. The Wrongs of the Indian.
110. Summer.
111. Night.
112. Death.
113. Revenge.
114. The Study of Geography.
115. Music.
116. The Moon.
117. The Stars.
118. Comets.
119. The Earth.
120. Day.
121. Autumn.
122. The Pleasures of Memory.
123. The Sabbath.
124. The Fifth Commandment.
125. Virtue.
126. Egypt.
127. Snow.
128. Mountains.
129. Forests.
130. Character of the Ancient Romans.
131. Our Country.
132. The Miser.
133. Oriental Countries.
134. Hope.
135. Life.
136. Rivers.
137. Astronomy.
138. Rain.
139. Vice.
140. Riches and Poverty.
141. The Fourth of July.
142. The Bible.
143. Morning.
144. The Art of Painting.
145. The Mahometan Religion.
146. The Applications of Steam.

181. "Whatever is, is right."
182. "Beware of desperate steps; the darkest day—
Live till to-morrow—will have passed away."
183. "There's a Divinity that shapes our ends,
Rough hew them how we may."
184. "Health is the vital principle of bliss."
185. "Heaven from all creatures hides the book of fate."
186. "Be it ever so homely, there's no place like home."
187. "Hypocrisy, the only evil that walks
Invisible except to God alone."
188. "Kings are earth's gods; in vice their law's their will,
And if Jove stray, who dares say, Jove doth ill."
189. "Sweet is the image of the brooding dove!
Holy as Heaven a mother's tender love!"
190. "The bolt that strikes the towering cedar dead,
Oft passes harmless o'er the hazel's head."
191. "Who by repentance is not satisfied,
Is nor of heaven, nor earth."
192. "Honor and shame from no condition rise;
Act well your part; there all the honor lies."
193. "Suspicion is a heavy armor, and
With its own weight impedes more than protects."
194. "Treason does never prosper."
195. "I love thee, twilight! for thy gleams impart
Their dear, their dying influence to my heart."
196. "True charity's a plant divinely nursed."
197. "Good name in man and woman
Is the immediate jewel of their souls."

198. "Sweet are the uses of adversity."
199. "Man yields to custom as he bows to fate,
    In all things ruled—mind, body, and estate."
200.   "Experience is the school
    Where man learns wisdom."
201. Honesty is the best policy.
202. All is not gold that glitters.
203. One to-day is worth two to-morrows.
204. Birds of a feather
    Flock together.
205. Great talkers, little doers.
206. Keep thy shop, and thy shop will keep thee.

ARGUMENTATIVE DISCOURSES.

When the subject is given in the form of a question, the pupil may take either side.

1. Is conscience in all cases a correct moral guide?
2. Do public amusements exercise a beneficial influence on society?
3. Does the study of the classics, or of mathematics, afford the better discipline to the mind?
4. Is a monarchy the strongest and most stable form of government?
5. Did the Crusades have a beneficial influence on Europe?
6. Do the learned professions offer as promising an opening to a young man as mercantile life?
7. Is a nation justified in rising against its rulers?
8. Is a lawyer justified in defending a bad cause?
9. Is it an advantage for a young man who intends to become a merchant to go through college?
10. Do parents or teachers exercise the greater influence in forming the character of the young?
11. Is it best for judges to be elected by the people?
12. Does the Pulpit or the Bar afford a better field for eloquence?
13. Does the reading of novels have a good or bad effect on the community?
14. Do inventions have a tendency to improve the condition of the laboring classes?
15. Is raffling at church fairs wrong?
16. Is the education of boys and girls in the same classes expedient?
17. Should there be a property qualification for suffrage?

THE END.